TWD III

TROUBLE WITH A DREAM III
Ezekiel 7:9 "In Pink"

by Penelope Wells

A tale based on the life and times of the artist Penelope Wells

GALVANIZED GROUP INC.

In order to protect the innocent, as well as the guilty, I have changed names and locations and am compelled to say that portions of the book are fictional. Some characters have been combined and timeframes altered; therefore, any similarity to persons living or dead is completely coincidental.

This is my story, written in my own words. I'm not what you'd call a professional writer, but I have been asked to recount the tales of my adventures to captivated friends and acquaintances ever since I was a tot.

After I was offered a movie deal and told that Hollywood was desperate for me, I decided that it was time to put pen to paper, and this is it… my story….

THE LETTER

Dear Pat,

    I'm writing to let you know that I'm on the run. I've shot four men, members of an outlaw motorcycle club. It was self-defense, but I doubt that the truth matters much right now. Things are chaotic, I'm certain that a hit man is on my trail and probably the FBI as well.

    I'm headed for a safe place; you know that I can survive. I'll see you when it's over.

          Love,

          Sissy

TABLE OF CONTENTS

MOBSTER MAYHEM

One fall afternoon, I got a call from my old high school friend, Marcia. I was thrilled to hear from her. We had lost contact with each other after she went away to college and it had been years since we had spoken.

Marcia told me that she was married and that her husband had a friend named Gordon who would like to meet me. "It's a perfect match!" Marcia exclaimed. "I know that he'll be crazy about you! You're just his type; he loves tall thin redheads. I have it all planned, you can marry Gordon and we will all be best friends together! We could see each other all the time!" She went on to explain that Gordon was an importer and was worth nearly two hundred million dollars!

"I have it all set up for two weeks from today, we can meet at Gordon's house on the beach in Malibu for the weekend; we'll have a great time. Please say you'll go, I really need to see you, I miss you so much!"

Marcia was so excited about it, even if I had wanted to say no I couldn't have, so I agreed to go for the weekend.

Two days before I was to leave for Malibu, Gordon called me from Africa. His safari was taking longer than expected and his return home had been delayed. He had already spoken to Marcia, she and her husband couldn't make it the following weekend when he would be available, but he still wanted me to come. I didn't feel comfortable going alone, so Gordon suggested that I bring a friend and I reluctantly agreed to make the trip.

As it turned out, I ended up taking a girl with me that I didn't know very well. Her name was Sheena, and she worked in the shop next to mine. She was the only one who could get the time off of work on such short notice.

Sheena was tall, like the Empire State Building, a pretty girl and sharp dresser. She was a bit crude, but seemed nice enough and she was anxious to go. I figured that it was better than having the pressure of being alone with Gordon right away.

When the time came to leave, I was a nervous wreck, and so was Sheena; after all, we were going to Malibu to spend the weekend with a multi-millionaire who we didn't even know. I wondered what kind of a man Gordon would be.

We decided to save the price of a drink on the plane and sneak on our own vodka and orange juice in plastic sport cups. Sheena mixed the drinks and I didn't pay any attention.

After we boarded the plane, I started to drink from my sports cup; the drink was strong, way too strong, but I didn't want to get a panic attack on the plane, so I sucked it down.

Sheena finished her drink and then ordered another. By the time we had reached altitude, she was already drunk and out of control; shouting obscenities and insults at the other passengers. She tried to get up to confront a man a few seats ahead of us who had told her to shut up, but she fell down, landed on me and spilled her drink in my boot. I was barelegged with a short dress on and the whole drink went down inside.

Sheena was a horrible mean drunk and so obnoxious that our fellow passengers began screaming for someone to throw her off of the plane. The frustrated flight attendants, agreed with the enraged passengers and said that they would be happy to throw her out, but they couldn't open the plane door or we would lose pressure.

I was drunk too, and sick besides. I wanted to help with Sheena, but all I could do was say, "Shut up Sheena," between bouts of throwing up. Sheena was uncontrollable and irate and by far the meanest drunk that I had ever seen.

After we landed and got off the plane, I didn't know how Sheena was still on her feet, but she was, and she headed straight for the bar. I tried to get her to stay with me to meet Gordon's driver at the pre-arranged meeting place, but she gave me a shove and said with a drunken slur, "Get out of my way, I need a drink."

My vision was impaired and I was literally seeing double, things seemed as though they were moving, and yet standing still at the same time. I felt weird, very weird, I had never been this drunk before. I knew that I was supposed to go outside and that's where I headed, toward the sunshine. With every step I took, I could hear the squish, squish, squish of the sticky orange juice and vodka in my boot. The sound echoed in my ears and the feeling of my toes beginning to stick together was actually scaring me. My mind was so confused that it seemed as though it was threatening my life.

I sat on a bench to wait for Gordon's car and tried to pull myself together. A concerned woman stopped and asked me if I was okay. I told her I was, even though I wasn't. I was embarrassed that I had been so

7

foolish to let myself get in this condition.

It wasn't long before Gordon's car pulled up and the driver helped me in. I told him where to find Sheena, but later wished I hadn't. The driver came out with her in tow, screaming and cussing that she didn't want to leave the bar.

In the car, Sheena smoked one cigarette after another, she was hanging her legs out the window and screaming at the driver to stop and buy her a drink. She was so out of it, that she was pawing me, putting her hands in my dress, grabbing my breasts and trying to kiss me. I kept knocking her off of me, time after time, listening to her scream at the driver, smelling the smoke and throwing up. With my toes sticking together in my wet boot, it was nearly driving me insane! What a miserable ride and the trip had only just begun.

When we got to Gordon's house, I laid down on the sofa and the driver got me a cool cloth for my head. He then went to the garage and began to unload the luggage.

Sheena went into the kitchen and opened the refrigerator, "I need a drink," I heard her shout. "Doesn't this asshole have any booze in this house?" Sheena belligerently rifled through the kitchen, throwing food and spilling milk and juices on the counters, floor and walls, while cursing and being cruel to the servants. And all I could do about it was lay there with my puke bag and rag on my head and say, "Shut up, Sheena."

Gordon came home shortly after our arrival, when he saw me lying on the sofa he came over and introduced himself. "My man tells me that you got airsick, I'm sorry to hear that." He sat on the edge of the sofa and began to talk to me, he seemed concerned. We spoke briefly, then we heard the sound of breaking glass, Sheena had thrown a bottle of catsup against the wall.

Gordon went into the kitchen and saw the horrible mess. He wasn't about to put up with this bitch, he grabbed her and tossed her out the front door and her bags after her.

I wouldn't have thought it possible, but in front of the house Sheena was even more disgusting and nasty than she had been before. As I lay on the sofa, I could hear the cursing and screaming. What a scene she was making, and Gordon was just as bad.

I had to do something; somehow I had to put an end to this! I struggled to my feet, planning to go outside and try to calm Sheena down. I made it to the door and as I began to walk outside, Gordon pushed me back into the house. He shoved me so hard that he knocked me down, "You're not going anywhere!"

"Gordon you've got to stop this!" I exclaimed. "Sheena's just drunk, she doesn't know what she's doing!"

"You're drunk too, but you're not acting like that, you're nice and sweet, there's no excuse for her!"

Well maybe it was true, that was no excuse for Sheena, but what was his excuse? He was acting just as bad as she was! Gordon wasn't drunk and he had pushed me and knocked me down, he was so angry at Sheena that he didn't even notice that he had done it. Now he was telling me how nice and sweet I was while I sat on the floor looking up at him. I might have been drunk, but still, I could see that something was very wrong with this man.

All of Gordon's neighbors came outside to see what the commotion was, and I recognized nearly every one of them from the media. They were looking at Sheena standing in the street, drunk and nasty with a huge pile of luggage, and I felt responsible. I wasn't sure what I should do; I couldn't think straight, but I tried to clear my head and figure out a solution. Staying in the house and leaving the drunken Sheena in the street wasn't an option. Who knows what would happen to her? And besides that, the people back home might hold me responsible if something horrible did befall her.

I had just managed to get back on my feet when I heard the phone ringing in the kitchen. No one else was paying attention, they were all in the front yard, so I decided to answer it and stumbled to the phone, "Hello."

There was a man on the other end of the line, "Hello, this is Ira; is Gordon available?"

I tried to call Gordon to the phone, but he wouldn't stop screaming at Sheena long enough to hear me. "What's all the shouting I hear? Is there a problem out there?" Ira asked.

I frantically told him that Gordon had thrown my friend out of the house. "It's so dark outside and she's drunk and she doesn't know what she's doing, and I'm drunk too and I'm dizzy and sick. I can't just leave her out there, but I don't know what to do about it!"

Ira had a nice voice, at that moment I didn't care who he was, I had to

9

find a way to get out of there and this seemed as good as any. Suddenly I heard myself ask, "Will you please come and get us?"

"Sure I'll come and get you," Ira answered enthusiastically. "It'll take me about forty-five minutes to get there; Gordon is pretty far up the beach."

After my conversation with Ira, I sat down and waited, and the fighting never stopped. Forty-five minutes later, a luxurious new Jaguar pulled up in front of Gordon's house and two men got out and began to load the luggage into the trunk. When Gordon saw what was going on, he was happy to get rid of Sheena, and assumed that I was staying with him. He assured me that his friend, Ira, was "more than safe" and that Sheena would be just fine.

Gordon got angry when he realized that I was planning to leave with Sheena and he tried to block the doorway and force me stay. I wanted to keep things as peaceful as possible, so I told him that I would see that Sheena was safe at a hotel, and then come back later. When Gordon still didn't move out of my way, it made me angry and I shoved him aside and walked out. I wanted to get the hell out of there!

Sheena and I climbed into the car with the two strangers, and as we were driving away Gordon yelled at the top of his lungs, "Vic will know how to handle you, bitch!"

Well, it certainly was true Ira's friend, Vic, did know how to handle Sheena, but I don't think that it was at all what Gordon had in mind. Vic had a rough raspy, deep voice with a heavy New York accent and he spoke in a slang that I had only heard in gangster movies, "Come ova here baby and tell me what happened back there." Vic was driving the car, he had his right arm resting on the back of the seat and he motioned for Sheena to move closer to him. He had a way of taking control and a command in his voice and Sheena did what he asked; she quickly scooted next to him and was more than happy to tell him all about it. She was still a mean nasty drunk, but Vic thought that she was funny. The more vulgar and disgusting she got, the more he liked it. Vic acted as though Sheena was performing a comedy routine and he was laughing at the punch lines.

Vic turned and looked at his friend in the back seat with me, "Hey Ira, can you believe this broad?" he said with a smile. Then he leaned back towards Sheena and snickered, "Tell me more baby, I find this very interesting."

What a relief, he could handle her and we weren't going to get kicked out on the side of the road, in the middle of nowhere.

Meanwhile, in the back seat, it was certainly no picnic. Ira was definitely not my idea of a dream man. He had a pudgy face and a big chunky belly. His shirt had bright colored, blue and green stripes that tightly stretched across it and he wore coke bottle lens glasses. When I looked through his glasses, at his magnified eyes, they seemed to ripple outward and outward like rings of water when you throw a stone into a pond. I had to look away because they made me dizzy.

Being unattractive was one thing, but what an obnoxious pest, Ira was pawing me and driving me nuts. I didn't want to be mean to him, after all, he had rescued us and that had earned him some latitude. So, instead of socking him in the chops and slamming him across the car, like I felt like doing, I politely kept prying his paws off of me. I wondered; where was the justice in this situation? Sheena should have been the one struggling with the obnoxious octopus in the back seat, instead of enjoying the attention of a fun attractive man.

While I was holding Ira off, I heard a roar from the front seat, it was Sheena, "I have a headache!" she screamed and cried.

"Would I ever get a break? Now is when we get kicked out," I dreaded. And worst of all, we were in a deserted area.

Sheena was screaming non-stop while Vic was driving the car. "Alright, alright," he said, "I'll get you some aspirin!" and then, he pulled into the parking lot of a store that was closed.

"Oh great here it comes," I whispered and then braced myself for the kick-out. I could picture the whole thing, Sheena being dragged from the car kicking and screaming, and me being left there with the bitch lying on the asphalt, making my life miserable. What would happen to us after that? I couldn't even speculate.

Vic got out of the car and I watched his every move; to my surprise, he didn't kick us out as I had expected he would. Instead, he walked to the store and pounded on the door. Someone was still inside and came to see what he wanted. They spoke briefly and then the man went to get some aspirin, he handed it to Vic as he locked the store and then left.

But that wasn't the end of the problem, Sheena needed water and we didn't have any; she continued to scream and cry until I thought my head would burst. Lucky for me, there happened to be one of those water-filter machines in front of the store, the kind that you bring your own gallon bottles to fill. Vic put in some change and the water began to flow.

I have to admit that it was funny watching Vic trying to get the aspirin down the drunken Sheena. She had to fit her head into the area where you fill the bottle and try to keep the aspirin in her mouth, while she sucked up the water and swallowed the aspirin; quite a feat for a drunken buffoon. Sheena kept dropping the aspirin from her mouth and falling down on the sidewalk. "Come on you crazy broad," Vic said. He was laughing as he grabbed her by the hair to help direct her a bit.

Sheena was drenched, water on her face, hair and lovely dress. Finally I heard her exclaim, "I got it!"

"Well at least that's over," I said in relief, "but I wonder what this obnoxious bitch going to do next?"

Vic and Sheena got back in the car and we traveled further down the road. I could see lights ahead; maybe we were coming to a town! There was no telling how much more of my wonderful friend these two guys were willing to put up with. At least if we were kicked out here, I could find a pay phone and call a cab, or maybe even get a hotel room.

Vic, pulled off the road, and into the parking lot of an elegant restaurant on the beach, "Let's get something to eat," he suggested.

We all agreed, climbed out of the car and went inside where we were quickly seated at a table. I ordered a Ginger ale and I couldn't believe it when Sheena ordered two Martinis! I tried to stop her, but there was just no reasoning with her.

The restaurant had a full ocean view; it was already dark, but the beach was well lit and we could see the white water crashing on the sand. It was beautiful and I could have enjoyed it except of course, for Ira the pest pawing on me.

By the time the drinks came, I was almost "half-witted" and realized that Sheena and I were with two strangers and maybe even in danger. I went to the ladies room and tried to call a friend in L.A. hoping that he would come and get us. I still felt very strange, my eyes wouldn't focus, and the numbers on the phone were moving around and fading into and crossing over each other. I kept dialing the wrong number and finally defeated, I had to give up. I was unable to even dial a telephone. I couldn't help myself and no matter how hard I tried, I couldn't think straight. I decided that I had to ride it out and hope for the best. Gordon did say that his friend was safe, but I was certain that it was just to make me feel better about letting Sheena leave with him. It wasn't much comfort to me now.

By the time I got back to the table, Sheena had already downed one Martini and was starting on the next. The food had been served, so I ate a few bites and started to feel a little bit better, but Sheena was still being a bitch. Would she ever stop? I could hardly stand it anymore; the sound of her loud drunken voice went right through me. I was already at wits end when she decided to target me with her nasty ugly mouth. "Penelope," she bellowed, "you're stupid. Do you guys want to know how stupid she is?"

"Sheena, shut up," I demanded.

"Don't you tell me to shut up, stupid. You're so stupid, you don't even know that you've been tripping. We were flying in the sky, tripping on our trip, ha, ha, ha!"

Suddenly I realized why I had been feeling so strange; my God, Sheena had drugged me!! All the things that she had put me through that day had driven me to the boiling point. The scene on the plane, the way that she had acted in the car on the drive to Malibu, trashing Gordon's house and fighting with him in front of the neighbors. And now, I find out that she had drugged me!

I tried to control myself and think things through. Was I going to sit here and let her brow beat me? Was that the only option that I had? I knew that Sheena wasn't going to stop until she had ground me into the dirt and maybe not even then. How does one behave in a civilized manner in a case like this, seated at a table in an elegant restaurant? If there was a proper way to behave, I couldn't think of it and I wasn't about to take a verbal beating from this big-mouthed bitch. I slammed my fist on the table, "Sheena you shut up or I'm going to make you shut up!"

It wasn't like me to give a warning and lose the element of surprise, but I did. I guess that I was hoping that she would take the warning and stop, but it was too much to ask for. Sheena didn't even hesitate and took another smart ass crack at me, and with it, she had pushed me far over the edge.

I stood up, reached across the table and grabbed her by the hair; I slammed Sheena's face down in her plate, BAM! Then I dragged her toward me over the tabletop. She was swinging her arms and screaming bloody murder. Food and drinks went flying everywhere.

Vic got up, he was laughing as he grabbed hold of Sheena. Ira pulled me back and then Vic stood Sheena up, holding her by the scruff of the neck. What a mess, she was covered in a rainbow of food and sauces with little chunks of clam sliding down her cheeks, and I started laughing with Vic.

The people dining at the restaurant were aghast, the manager and waiters came rushing over to our table, but when they saw Vic, they hesitated. "Who is this guy anyway?" I wondered.

"The girls just need some fresh air," Vic told them. He still had Sheena by the back of the neck and started to walk her through the restaurant toward the door; laughing the whole time. I was glad that Vic agreed with me and thought that it was funny.

Ira and I weren't far behind and when Vic got to the door, he looked back at Ira, "Let's keep the girls apart for a while, they need some time to cool off." Then Vic looked at me and smiled, "And I thought that I was just going out for a quiet business dinner with my attorney tonight. Let's take a walk on the beach; Ira you two go that way."

When Vic dragged Sheena away in the opposite direction, I heard her screaming, "Penelope, you bitch, look what you did to me!"

"Shut up Sheena," Vic said laughing, "you deserved it. You're lucky I was there or Penelope would have kicked the shit out of you!"

Would I ever see Sheena again? I certainly hoped not. Where was he taking her? If I was lucky, Vic was a murderer and he would kill her, cut her body into pieces and feed her to the sharks. But no, that was only a pleasant fantasy.

When I reached the sand, I slowly walked to the edge of the water and tried to calm myself down, but unfortunately, it was impossible with stupid Ira still smashed up against me. There were musicians playing stringed instruments on the beach and they began to softly serenade us. I guess if a person didn't know any better, they could think that Ira and I were lovers, instead of what it really was, a nauseous drugged woman warding off an obnoxious octopus. I couldn't believe that it was actually happening! How much grosser could it get?!

I was a bit shaky and I sat down on the sand. Ira saw this as his big chance, and he wrapped his arms around me and pulled me toward him, trying to make me lay down on him. I was face to face with Ira, looking into those huge magnifying glasses, the light caught them and his eyes started rippling bigger and bigger! "Ira I'm getting dizzy!" I warned, and I tried to push him away. But Ira didn't let go, he clenched onto me even tighter and … BARF…. I threw up all over him. Ira jumped up and ran away. "I wish I would have thought of that sooner!" I said to myself.

I sat quietly on the beach, watching the waves lapping on the sand; the cool fresh air was wonderful and I wasn't in any hurry to leave. I was finally getting some peace and planned to sit there until I came down enough to at least make a phone call. I was in a safe area and as long as I got to the phone before the restaurant closed, it would be alright. I didn't care about Sheena, my luggage or anything else, I just needed to get my mind back.

As I sat there trying to pull it together, I saw a man walking toward me. I didn't know who it was; I just hoped that it wasn't Ira. I decided that I wasn't going to take anymore crap from him and I grabbed a handful of sand and waited; if he tried to grope me, I planned to shove it in his face and give him a swift kick.

I was pleased when the man came into view, and I saw that it was Vic. He slowly approached, and sat down in the sand next to me. "I must apologize for my friend," he said in his deep sexy voice. "He's a great attorney, but he can be a little, how should I say… over-zealous at times. He's completely harmless, but I'm sorry that I so foolishly subjected you to him. Anyway, how you feeling, baby?"

"Not too good," I admitted.

"Yes, I can definitely understand that. Not that I have experienced it personally for myself, but I've heard that some of those hallucinogenic drugs can be, well, not so terrific."

"It's definitely not so terrific."

Vic, reached over and held my hand, "You're shaking," he said concerned. He took off his suit jacket and put it around my shoulders, then started to lift me to my feet. "Come on baby, let me get you a room where you can get some rest, it's too cold for you to be sitting out here on the beach in that little dress."

"Wait a minute," I stopped him, "I don't want to put up with Sheena or Ira anymore, I'd rather stay here and freeze."

"Don't worry," Vic assured me, "it's all been taken care of. Sheena passed out on the sand and I threw her in the back seat with Ira."

When we got to the car, Vic, opened the driver side door and helped me in. I saw Ira and Sheena in the back seat together, and it was hysterical. Ira was sitting there with a sour look on his face, his shirt was wet and stained and Sheena had dried food and sand sticking to her face and clothes. She was slobbering and pawing all over Ira, pulling at his pants and trying to unbutton them while Ira kept pushing her off.

This time, I was the one in the front seat sitting next to Vic, with his arm around me. As we rode down the winding road, I listened to Sheena moan and complain, she was putting her hand in her panties, being obscene and making Ira miserable. The whole thing was ghastly but still, I smiled, it seemed that justice had been served after all.

Fortunately, it wasn't long before, Vic, pulled up to an impressive hotel. The valet opened the door and Vic and I started to walk inside. When they pulled, Sheena, out of the car, she was sloppy and slobbery. I asked, Vic, what we were going to do with her, "I certainly don't want to share a room with her," I firmly stated.

"Don't worry, we'll put her in the back until she sobers up, and then take her to the airport."

Vic, had no sooner finished his sentence when, Sheena, pulled down her panties. "I've got to pee!" she loudly announced, and then let it rip, in front of everyone, right at the entrance of the luxurious hotel! Ira, tried to stop her, but the pee ran out in a river, down the sidewalk and over the curb.

Vic, was mortified, "Throw that pig in the dumpster!!" he shouted. Immediately, the men picked, Sheena, up and threw her in the dumpster, she and all of her luggage. I didn't try to intervene, I didn't bat an eye, as far as I was concerned, drunk or not, Sheena, was finally where she belonged, with the rest of the trash.

Ira, got back in the Jag and went to park it while, Vic, and I waited for the elevator. "I hope that didn't disturb you," Vic apologized. "A lady such as yourself, should never have to witness such a disgusting scene."

After fighting with, Sheena, in the restaurant, I was surprised that, Vic, had referred to me as a lady; apparently it hadn't fazed him. He was certainly very different from any of the "men" that I had met in the past few years.

Vic and I held hands in the elevator and he inserted a special key for it to go all the way to the top floor. We were starting to walk down the hall, when I realized that I had neglected to check in and give the hotel clerk my credit card. "Oh no! What was in store for me next on this torture trip? Was, Vic, taking me to his room and assuming that he was getting laid?" That was definitely not in my plan for the night! I started to tense up, "Vic, I forgot to give my credit card to the clerk. We better go back down!"

"That's okay baby, forget about it."

That wasn't what I wanted to hear, I was just about to break away from him and go back to the desk, when, Vic, opened the door to a lovely room. "Here's your room," he announced, "I hope it meets your expectations. And I'm right next door, in case you need me."

I walked inside and Vic followed, "Well, what do ya think, classy ain't it? You like the orchids, huh? They're beautiful flowers, I'll have them put fresh ones in for ya in the morning. What's your favorite color?"

"Pink, I guess."

"I should have guessed, a feminine color for such a gorgeous feminine woman. Now, come over here and have a look at the bathroom. What do you think of this baby, a Jacuzzi bathtub? Yeah, I can just picture you, relaxing in that tub full of bubbles."

"It's very nice, Vic, but this room is too expensive for me."

"Don't insult me, like I said before, forget about it. Now I wanna know, you gonna be okay in here by yourself tonight? I mean, with that pig drugging you and all, it might get rough, like I said before, not so terrific."

I tried to herd, Vic, toward the door, "I'll be okay, I think it's finally wearing off. If I could just get some sleep, I think I'll be fine."

"Nobody needs to hit me over the head with a hammer," Vic said before he stepped into the hall, "but remember, I'm right in the next room and I can be in here in a flash! And baby, another thing, I've got business to take care of tomorrow, but I'd love to take ya out tomorrow night and show ya a good time. Maybe make up for some of the unpleasantness inflicted on ya tonight."

"That would be nice." I thanked, Vic, for everything and slowly closed the door.

Vic, was a very tempting man and he definitely wasn't intimidated by me. I wondered what I would think of him in the light of day.

The next morning, I slept in and then ordered room service. A few minutes later, three waiters came into the room in a flurry, with a lovely tray of delicious food and huge bouquets of pink orchids. I was pleasantly surprised and thoroughly enjoyed it; it had been a good long while since I had had any special attention.

I savored every bite of breakfast, and when I finished I got up, opened the draperies and beheld a breathtaking view. I might not have been in Malibu, but where I had landed was definitely nothing to complain about! I was at the beach, and decided to get outside and enjoy it while I could. I was still going out with Vic that night, but planned to return home first thing the next morning.

When I walked past the front desk, I stopped and asked about Sheena. I was told that they had rousted her at sunrise and taken her to the airport. "Don't concern yourself with her miss, Mr. Valente, left orders that you are not to be bothered with any unpleasantness."

I was glad that the bitch was gone and when I walked toward the door, the concierge tried to have an attendant come to the beach with me to carry my belongings and wait on me. But I didn't want anything to do with it, I just wanted to be alone and enjoy the sunshine. It was fall, the weather at home was already cold, but in L.A. it was still warm and sunny and I considered it a real treat.

When I reached the beach, I wiggled my toes in the sand and laid in the sun for an hour or so, then I walked down the beach and up to the pier. I watched the men fishing for a while and then browsed the cute shops. I had a nice seafood lunch at a quaint little restaurant and felt content. "At least I got one good day out of this trip," I consoled myself.

Later, I returned to the hotel and Vic, called me on the phone, to firm up our date. I told him that he could pick me up in about an hour. I would have preferred to spend the night alone, relaxing in the luxurious hotel, but I felt that I at least owed, Vic, the courtesy of keeping my word to him.

As I started to prepare for my date, I braced myself for the worst; this trip had been such a nightmare, I didn't know what horror would befall me next! I wondered if I had been hallucinating the night before, and just imagined that, Vic, was handsome and charming. Would I find that he was actually a strange-looking weirdo?

I had a lovely new dress that I had bought for the trip, and since this would be my only chance, I decided to wear it. I had already fixed my hair and makeup and as I was putting on my jewelry, I heard a commotion outside. I walked to the window to see what was going on, and saw an incredible stretch limo pulling up in front of the hotel; it must have been as long as a bus! I recognized the hood ornament, it was some kind of a Mercedes sports car. "There must be a big shot or movie star staying here tonight," I presumed and then waited to see what famous person would emerge from the outrageously expensive car. When the chauffer got out and then opened the door, I was shocked to see, Vic, getting out of the back seat!

"I'm sure glad that I wore my best dress!" I whispered, and nervously ran to the mirror to make sure that I was put together. My new dress was jet black, clingy, and fell off the shoulder. My jewelry and shoes glittered and my eyes were bright with excitement. I picked up my crystal perfume bottle and walked through a spray of expensive French perfume, then I sat down and waited for Vic.

Soon, I heard a knock at the door. I waited a minute to get my composure, then I got up, held my breath, and opened it.

I'm not sure, but I think that I may have gasped when I saw Vic standing there, it was his eyes, they were stunning, hazel with flecks of glistening gold that sparkled in the light. Tall and muscular, Vic, had sandy brown hair and a soft neatly-trimmed beard.

He smiled, stood in the doorway and just stared at me, "Baby, give me a minute, I have to pick my jaw up off the floor, you're absolutely gorgeous!"

Vic was the most charming man that I had ever met; he made such a big deal out of me, that within the first two minutes of seeing him, he had already made me feel better than I had in years! I was incredibly happy, Vic, was definitely no strange-looking weirdo!

I grabbed my little evening bag, and we headed out of the hotel. By the time we got down to the car, it was surrounded by people, gawking and asking questions. The chauffer cleared the way and Vic and I climbed inside.

"Who are you? Who are you?" the curious onlookers kept shouting. It was a valid question; I would have liked to know the answer myself. Really; who is this guy?

When I sat inside the incredible car, I left plenty of room between Vic and myself, but he didn't like it. He reached behind me and put his hand on my hip, "Come ova here baby," he said, and he slid me across the leather seat, close beside him.

I started to giggle, "Vic, I can't believe it, you're actually intimidating me!" After all the times that I had been told how scary I was, this man was actually intimidating me! Suddenly, I didn't feel like a scary monster anymore and it was wonderful to be free of the dark negative feeling about myself.

Vic didn't acknowledge that I had said anything to him, he held me close and gave me a passionate kiss. I had never had a man kiss me like that before, he was so powerful, so strong, I felt completely dominated by him. Vic gently pushed my hair out of my eyes, and looked at me intently, "You're gorgeous baby," he said in a low growl. One kiss and I was under his spell.

"There's a nice place just up the road," Vic told me, "makes a delicious cheesecake. You like cheesecake baby?"

I couldn't think for a second, but then answered, "Yeah sure… sure I like cheesecake."

We pulled up to the restaurant in the long sleek car and before we could even get out, people were already gathering around it.

Vic and I quickly got out and entered the restaurant. After we were seated, he order a bottle of fine wine. "Excellent choice sir," the waiter complemented him.

"Well baby, bet you didn't know that you were out with a high-class guy tonight. I know all about wine. You being from wine country, I figured you would appreciate the finer things."

"I might be from wine country Vic, but I'm not crazy about wine, actually, I'd prefer a shot of whiskey."

Vic looked at me, he smiled and nodded, "A woman after my own heart. Make that two shots of whiskey."

I had never told, Vic, that I was from wine country. With my background, tripping on drugs or not, I knew that I would never divulge personal information about myself. That was a rule that was deeply ingrained in me, and I was certain that I hadn't even told him my last name. It was clear that, Vic, had done some inquiring about me and I suspiciously wondered why.

But, that concern didn't last, and it wasn't long before I had recklessly thrown caution to the wind. Vic and I were eating and drinking and having a wonderful time. He was different than any man that I had ever met before. I found that I was with someone who was actually doing the talking and entertaining me, and I loved it! I sat back and listened to Vic tell me incredible exciting tales of his dangerous shady escapades. It was obvious that, Vic, was a bad boy, but it truly didn't matter to me, this was my one and only night to have a good time and I wasn't going to blow it by over-concerning myself with his character. Who knew when I would even have the opportunity to go out with a man again? After tonight, it was all over; the next morning, it was back to my dreary meager life, and I decided that I wasn't going to waste a minute of this good time.

When we finished eating, Vic wanted to go dancing. As we left the restaurant and went to the car, the chauffer cleared the way, and we rushed inside. I didn't know where we were going next, just that we were headed inland. I wasn't concerned about it though, if Vic had something sinister up his sleeve, he had already had plenty of opportunity to follow through with it. I figured that he was out to have fun, the same as I was.

The ceiling of the limo was a huge mirror, surrounded by twinkling lights. Vic and I were looking at ourselves, laughing and making out, all the way to the nightclub. When we were getting close, there was a line of people that went all the way around the block, waiting to enter the club. I rolled down the window to get a closer look. "Vic, maybe we should go someplace else, I don't want to wait in that line."

"Don't worry about it baby."

The driver slowed down, and the crowd of people quickly left their place in line to gather around the car, anxiously waiting to see who would emerge. Then when the chauffer opened the door…..I got out! The crowd started roaring and taking pictures, so I posed for them.

When, Vic, got out behind me, he picked me up, "Let's give them a real show baby," and he put me on top of the car.

I seductively posed as the many cameras flashed and snapped one picture after another. Vic was laughing and encouraging the excitement. I heard him say, "She's gorgeous ain't she?"

When I had had enough, Vic, helped me down from the car, but he didn't put me on the ground, he threw me over his shoulder and carried me inside the nightclub. I waved to everyone as we went inside.

The club owner was waiting at the door and directed us to a table. I could see the waiters quickly rousting the other people away, making them give up their table for us. Vic and I were given the royal treatment; we drank whiskey and danced until we were out of breath.

We were headed back to the table, from the dance floor, when, Vic, picked me up again, "Dance for me baby," he said as he placed me on the tabletop. I shimmied my shoulders and wildly tossed my hair. The whole nightclub was clapping and cheering as I danced like a crazed go-go dancer. Vic leaned back in his chair, "She's gorgeous ain't she," I heard him say again.

When my lively dance reached a fever pitch, Vic stood up and I jumped into his arms. He fell back on the floor and we started wildly making out and groping each other. Vic paused and looked in my face, "It's time for us to leave," he said with a smile, and we got up and left the nightclub in a flurry of shouts and applause.

And that's how the night went, we traveled from nightclub to nightclub, always going to the front of the line and being seated at the best table. People were asking to have their pictures taken with us, and still I wondered… who is this guy?

Vic and I stayed until the clubs closed, and then we climbed into the limo. We collapsed in the seat laughing and holding hands. "Thank you for showing me such a terrific time," I said sweetly and kissed his knuckles. I wanted to go on and tell him how much it had really meant to me, how miserable and lonely my life was, but I didn't. "Let him remember me the way he does now, exciting and gorgeous."

When we reached the hotel, Vic, kissed me goodnight at the door and then went to his room. Somehow, he thought that I was a lady. He respected me and didn't try to get laid. It surprised me, especially after our wild date, but I was grateful that I hadn't had to deal with the pressure.

The next morning, I got up early and planned to sneak out of the hotel and head for the airport. I packed my bags and heard a knock at the door. I thought that it was the porter, but I was wrong, it was Vic, "Baby, what are you doing to me? Trying to leave without even saying good-bye? You're breaking my heart baby." Vic put his hand on his chest and acted like he was ready to collapse.

"I'm sorry, Vic, I didn't want to see you before I left, I thought that it would be easier this way."

"You can't leave without having breakfast, let me at least take you out to breakfast."

Vic was a very persuasive man, and I agreed to go to breakfast. The next thing I knew, he had persuaded me to go boating with him and then later, I found myself dressing to go out with him again that night. Before I knew it, three days had passed and I found myself in the Jaguar with, Vic, on our way to look at RV's. I had mentioned to him that I liked the mountains and that I enjoyed hiking in the tall trees, swimming in the cold streams and lying in the warm sun. He wanted to take me on a mountain trip, but preferred to go in style; roughing it didn't appeal to, Vic.

When we arrived at the RV dealership and were browsing the lot, a salesman was hovering over us. Vic gave him a disapproving glare, "Hey, I don't appreciate you up my ass. If I need you for something, I'll ask." Vic didn't have much patience, or tact.

The two of us went from one vehicle to another, looking and trying to decide which one we wanted. Then, we entered a motor home that was as big as a bus, and of course that was the one that, Vic, liked. We looked at all of the special features and then headed down the narrow hallway toward the back bedroom. We both tried to pass through the doorway at the same time and found ourselves face to face, pressed up against each other. I felt a rush and I knew that my face was turning red. Vic placed both of his hands on the wall on each side of me, closing me in, then he growled in a deep breathy voice. He looked at me with those golden eyes, like a dangerous hungry lion.

When Vic grabbed hold of me, passion took me over and I went completely out of control. I savagely ripped open his shirt as he pushed me on the bed. Vic was a wild man, he roared and growled and tore off my dress. His soft beard tickled my neck and I shivered all over. I couldn't wait to have him and he knew it, "Beg for it baby, beg me for my cock!"

There wasn't a decision to be made, I wanted him like I had never wanted a man before and I begged, I begged him for his cock. "Give it to me, Vic! Now! I want it now!"

Vic reached down to pull off my panties and before he could even touch me, I was already beside myself; I screamed and pulled his hair!

Vic and I didn't make love, we fucked, he had turned me into a wild primal animal! I felt as though I was in a trance, existing in a place of complete carnal pleasure. I didn't even know where I was, and I didn't care! I kicked and screamed and clawed and had one orgasm after another! I didn't even know that men like, Vic, existed!

When we finally came back down to reality, the salespeople were pounding on the door, "What's going on in there? Open this door!"

When my eyes came back into focus, I saw that I was holding a handful of Vic's hair, and that I had kicked out the back window of the motor home. When Vic got up, he had bloody claw marks up and down his back and across his butt. "Vic I'm sorry!"

"Hey baby, don't apologize for showing me the time of my life! Come on, get yourself together, we've got to get out of here before the cops show up!"

My panties were torn to shreds and there was no way that I could put them back on. I tried to get into my dress, but it was ripped up too and didn't cover me very well.

"Oh no, no, I don't want anyone seeing you like that!" Vic said shaking his head. He took off his shirt and gave it to me, the buttons were missing, but at least I was covered. Vic grabbed my dress and panties and we hurriedly rushed past the salesmen. Vic threw some money at them, "That will cover the broken window," he said, and we ran to the car and dashed away.

Vic was driving with no shirt on, his hair was wet and his strong chest and arms were shiny and glistening. His big muscles flexed with every move he made.

I put my hand on his bulging bicep and lightly ran my fingers up and down the tight firm muscle, then, I reached for his chest and moved my hand downward. "Okay, baby, I'm pulling over!"

Immediately, Vic screeched the car to the side of the road. I leaned back on the seat and opened the shirt I was wearing, exposing my lustful body. Vic lunged toward me and began to kiss and lick me all over, "Oh baby, you taste so good!"

Vic and I had passionate sex on the side of the road and it wasn't long before I wanted him again. He was a man of steel, my perfect mate, it was a shame that I couldn't keep him.

Vic stayed in my room at the hotel that night, he got into bed and held his arms out to me, "Come over here baby, come and lay in my arms."

I climbed into bed beside him and rested my head on his strong muscular chest. Vic held me close and before I knew it, we had both fallen sound asleep. I had been alone for such a long time; it was comforting just to have someone close.

The next morning, the phone was ringing. "You might as well answer it

Vic, it's not for me, nobody knows that I'm here," I said shaking him awake.

Vic answered the phone, "Oh, hi Boss, uh yeah, I was planning on staying a few more days. You see, I met this super high-class broad."

"Well, I don't know, we were going camping."

"Yeah, camping, can you believe it? This broad already has me wrapped around her little finger."

"Oh, that important huh?"

At that point, I could see that Vic was needed at work and I signaled to him to forget about the camping trip. "Vic, the trip isn't that important, I don't want to interfere with your job."

Vic covered the mouthpiece of the phone with his hand, "I have to go back to Vegas," he told me, "you can just go with me."

"Sure I'll go to Vegas," I agreed, and the next thing I knew I was headed for Las Vegas in the Mercedes Limo. I wanted to see, Vic, as much as I could; I had to kind of "fill up my tank," so to speak. The passion and fun would soon be over and I had to get enough to last me for a long, long, while.

The Mercedes Limo didn't belong to Vic, it was owned by The Big Boss. Vic had come to L.A. to take care of some business and pick up the custom car. The boss owned the hotel where we had stayed at the beach and also one of the largest hotel casinos in Vegas. Vic worked and lived at the Vegas casino.

When we arrived in Vegas, we went up to Vic's room, "I had the girls move me to a bigger suite, I want you to have the best of everything!" he announced. And I happily shared the suite with him.

Even though I had spent more than my share of time in Las Vegas, I had never had any fun there. To me, Vegas represented a difficult and stressful, work place, but now, I was seeing it in a whole new light. Vic showed me the full Vegas experience. We saw all of the extravagant shows, gambled with thousands of dollars and in between, we tore the bedroom apart! I was having the time of my life!

Vic always introduced me to his friends as a, super high-class broad, and I had to grin each time I heard him say it. His friends all called him Vicious Vic, they were a rugged, tough-looking bunch, all with colorful nicknames; Thumbs Tambora, Inky Baldache and The Ratchet, to name a few. Unrestrained by rules or social formality, Vic and his friends said and did what other people only wished they could. They had a freedom that I had never experienced before, freedom and power. After being judged and restricted for so long, it was a potent aphrodisiac.

I was able to extend my trip for three more days, but the time quickly flew by and Vic tried to talk me into quitting my job and staying even longer. With my panic attacks, I was lucky that I had a job at all and I couldn't jeopardize it. I packed my bags, and then Vic reluctantly drove me to the airport.

As it turned out, my plane had been delayed for an hour, so Vic and I sat in the bar and talked. It surprised me when he began to bare his soul and told me that he had robbed a bank. "We had eighteen people on the floor and it still went off without a hitch, yeah, it was a great plan," he gloated. "I was spending the money and living it up like a king, didn't have a care in the world until Chooch Nicoletti got busted on an unrelated charge. I knew that there was a reason that we all called him Chooch, (Italian for jackass). Chooch sold us out to the authorities, and I was convicted. Well, I did my time and when I got released, I wasn't sure exactly what I was going to do, when Thumbs called and said that they could use my talents here in Las Vegas. I was glad to get out of New York and get a fresh start."

Vic paused for a moment and took a deep breath; he hesitated, but then went on, "I was in the penitentiary when my sweet mother passed away. I was her pride and joy and they said that she died of a broken heart. The guilt nearly killed me, but it gave me a reason to change my life. They say that Jesus is lost in prison, because so many people seem to find him there, but in my case it was true. I did find Jesus in prison, and I plan to see my mother again someday in heaven. I go to church three times a week," then he laughed, "except of course, since you've been here corruptin' me. I plan to stay totally legit from here on out, and in Las Vegas it won't be hard. What you go to prison for in other states, you're admired for here in Sin City."

I was surprised to hear that Vic considered himself a Christian, and I told him that I was a Christian too. "Oh no," he exclaimed, "a redhead and a Christian, now I'm hooked for sure. Ya know baby, every one of my wives was a redhead, I'm powerless against youse." We both laughed and then Vic got serious. "I'm not joking baby, I hafta see ya again."

"I'd like to see you again too, Vic. I'll let you know when I can take more time off work."

"No, that'll take too long, forget about that measly job. I'll come up with a truck and haul ya back."

I must admit that I was tempted, especially now that I knew that Vic was a Christian and was totally legitimate. He certainly didn't have any commitment problems, and it would have been great to escape my meager existence. But, on the chance of going from the frying pan into the fire, I told him no. I knew that I had to find out more about this shady character before I could trust him that far. My life might not have been the greatest, but at least I wasn't living it in prison.

After I got home, things were even more miserable at work than they had been before. As I expected, Sheena, had turned the whole story around and made me out to be the bad guy. Her friends at the shopping center were angry at me and after they had a few drinks at lunch, Sheena, and her band came into the jewelry store to challenge me. I managed to hold myself back, but I knew that it was only a matter of time before I would lose my temper. Lucky for me, Al was a good friend and he knew what the real story was with Sheena, at least I didn't have to worry about being fired.

Vic called me every night, and it helped me to get through the dreary workday. He really seemed to care, and I missed him very much. Time would tell, I would just take it slow and easy and see if he committed a crime. If he were legit as he claimed he was, it would make all the difference.

It had only been a short time since I had returned home from my vacation, when two men in suits came into the jewelry store looking for me. They flashed their badges; it was the FBI, and they wanted to ask me a few questions. I was concerned of course, and took them outside to an isolated picnic area where we could talk in private.

The agents grilled me about Vic. How did we meet? Where did we go and who did we see? I told them the story of how we met. I wasn't going to lie and I couldn't have cared less about what Gordon thought. From that point on, I was vague; after all, I really didn't know anything. We had gone to some nightclubs in Hollywood and then gambled in Vegas and seen a few shows, that was it.

The FBI men weren't satisfied with my answers and they kept pressing me for more information. Finally, exasperated, I said, "If this guy is the slick criminal that you seem to think he is, why in the world would he tell anything to some dumb girl, that he just met? It wouldn't make a bit of sense. And why are you investigating him anyway? What has he done?"

After that, the agents loosened up and told me that they weren't after Vic, they said that they were after The Big Boss. I believed that they were telling me the truth, and then asked if they thought it was safe for me to continue to see Vic. "We can't advise you miss, but just be careful the next time you meet a good looking man." They went on to tell me that they would be watching me, and that I now had an open file with the FBI. Before they left, one of the agents gave me his card, "If you think of anything, give me a call."

I watched them walk away and as they did, I heard one of them say, "Vicious Vic Valente, fresh out of the pen and working in Las Vegas, he must be the enforcer." The two men got into their car, it was unmarked but had the special lights.

When I got back to the jewelry store, I decided to check it out. I looked up the phone number for the FBI and found that it was the same number on the card that the men had given me. When I called it and asked for the agents, I was told that they were in the field and was promptly connected to their voicemail. It was true, the men were definitely from the FBI!

The episode was disconcerting, and I knew that I had to end it with Vic. Things were going exactly the way that I had feared they would. I was being dragged into something criminal that I knew nothing about, and now the FBI was watching me.

That night, when Vic called, I felt that I owed it to him to let him know that the FBI had questioned me, and I told him everything. Before I could go on to tell him that it was over between us, he said that he had to call the boss. "I'll ring ya back baby," and then quickly hung up the phone.

During the time that I was waiting for Vic to call me back, I was a little worried. Had telling him really been the right thing to do? I had known enough outlaw bikers to know the protocol; you were expected to give your friends a heads up if you knew something. But maybe these guys would see me as a liability. I was starting to freak out when Vic finally called back.

"Baby, you done the right thing by telling me about the FBI. I hope that they didn't scare ya, but don't worry about it, it's really nothing. The boss says that they're after him on some real estate deal, an establishment that he sold over three years ago, it's just a lot of bull. Now, I'm sorry baby, but I can't talk no more, I got business to take care of tonight and I'm already late. I'll call ya tomorrow. And don't forget, I don't want nobody else looking at those gorgeous legs."

After I hung up the phone, I started coughing. I had been fighting off a cold all week, and now, I had a high fever. I drank some water and was getting ready to go to bed when the doorbell rang. I peeked out the window and saw that it was the girl who lived in the apartment under me. She was holding a bucket in her hand and had a disgusted look on her face. There was always something going wrong with the old broken-down house and I figured that this was just one more thing for me to deal with.

"What's wrong now, Nadine?" I asked.

Nadine was a sweet woman, but an obvious drug addict. She was bone thin, her teeth were rotten and she had a hollow sunken look to her. "Do you have water up here?" she asked.

I invited her in and found that I had water. "Okay if I use your bathroom?" she asked.

"Sure, go ahead," I agreed, and she went into the bathroom. Nadine, filled her bucket with water and asked if she could come back in the morning and take a shower.

"Sure, Nadine, but maybe the landlord will have it fixed by then, he can't leave you without water."

"You mean the slumlord, don't you? You know how it goes around here, he never fixes anything and when he does, it's not done right and it takes forever."

"Yeah, you're right, I'll expect you in the morning," I agreed, and then I started to cough uncontrollably.

"Penelope, you don't look too good. Are you okay?" Nadine asked as she felt my forehead. "You're burning up; do you want me to take you to the emergency room?"

"Thanks, Nadine, but I'll be fine. You better get out of here before you catch it from me. I'll leave the door open for you in the morning, I don't think that I'm going to make it to work tomorrow."

Nadine left and I went to bed. When the cold of night set in, breathing the brisk air made me cough even harder, and I decided to splurge and turn on the heat. After a short while, I fell into a deep dark sleep.

In the morning, Nadine came up to take her shower and the door wasn't open for her. She pounded and pounded and when I didn't respond she walked around to my bedroom window and knocked loudly on that. She could see me through a crack in the window trim, lying motionless on the bed. Knowing that I was ill, she dialed 911.

When the police and emergency medical people arrived, they forced the door open and found the house full of carbon monoxide, from the faulty heating system. They dragged me out into the fresh air and resuscitated me. I don't remember anything until I woke up in the hospital with an oxygen mask on my face. Immediately, I had a fit-like spell, it felt like someone was forcing a red-hot poker through my veins and then my muscles began to convulse. When that terrifying fit ended, it was only a short time before another one began.

The hospital kept me for a few hours, but when they found out that I didn't have health insurance, they said that I was stable and released me. Before I left the hospital, I asked to speak to the doctor who had treated me. I asked him if I could stay until the fits went away, and he said that they wouldn't end up with unpaid hospital bills. He told me that I was suffering brain and nerve damage from carbon monoxide poisoning and that I would never recover. He said that there hadn't been any testing done on the long-term effects of carbon monoxide poisoning on humans, but that animal testing had been done, and that none of the animals had ever shown any improvement. "It's a miracle that you lived at all, just be grateful for that," he coldly told me and then walked out of the room. Minutes later, the orderly put me in a cab, and closed the door behind me.

When I got home, a man from the gas company was waiting there. He couldn't enter the basement where the furnace was located because the landlord had it locked with a heavy hasp and padlock. The next door neighbor came over to see what the problem was, and then went home to get his burgle tools and cut off the lock for me.

The man from the gas company entered the basement and found that the chimney was completely blocked with old broken mortar. He told me that the floor furnace and the hot water heater were vented to the chimney and that they were both filling the house with toxic products of combustion, year round. He red-tagged the furnace and the hot water heater and shut them down.

All this time, I had assumed that it had been the panic attacks causing my symptoms, but in reality, I was being poisoned by carbon monoxide...

being poisoned for all those years! No wonder I hadn't recovered from the panic disorder! No wonder I had problems!"

I climbed into bed and as I laid there, I remembered how I had "panic attacks" when I came home at night, and how they were always worse when I sat in my recliner, my recliner that was positioned right by the furnace. I thought about how the attacks had always gotten worse in the wintertime. The headaches, the tingling in my toes and fingers, dizziness and trouble breathing, it all added up!

I had no reason to suspect the furnace, I had called the landlord and asked him to check it because it smelled like dirt whenever it was turned on. He said that his handyman had thoroughly inspected it and he assured me that the furnace was fine and working properly. He concluded that the house was just old and that the smell would eventually go away. Carbon monoxide is odorless, so I must have been smelling the old broken mortar blocking the venting.

This was the most terrifying day of my entire life. I was having one attack after another, my body was convulsing, it felt like hot coals were pulsing through my veins and I was burning up with a high fever, coughing and struggling to breathe.

The sun went down and it was starting to get dark, as I turned on the bedroom light, I wondered how long I would be able to pay the electric bill. It was obvious that I wouldn't be able to work. I was knocked down for the count and I couldn't get back up, the doctor told me that I would never get well and I was scared, scared down to my very core. I had never experienced fear like I did that day, as I suffered one terrifying painful attack after another. Was this the way that I was going to have to live for the rest of my life? According to the doctor, it was.

I was crying in my pillow when Vic called. He could tell that I was upset and immediately asked me what was wrong. When I told, Vic, that I had been poisoned by carbon monoxide, and what the doctor had said, he was shocked. "Baby, don't pay attention to what that that crazy doctor told you, he sounds like a quack to me. I'll get you a specialist; you're going to be just fine. I'll pick up a truck and leave tonight to come and get ya. I should be there with the guys, sometime in the morning. And don't worry baby, I love ya."

Vic loved me and he was coming to get me! Criminal or not, he cared and was going to help!

In the morning, Vic showed up with Thumbs and a few other guys that I hadn't met before. They had a big truck and began to pack and load my belongings. I told them just to take my personal items and leave everything else for Nadine, since she had saved my life.

Vic stayed until he had everything organized, and then the two of us got in my Porsche to leave. I looked up at the old house that I had been living in, and as we pulled away, I felt like I was being unchained from a dark dreary dungeon, where I had nearly been tortured to death. Now, it was time for me to move on to my new life. Even though I knew that I was facing many difficult challenges, I was still hopeful.

Vic kept his word and found me an excellent doctor. This doctor didn't just give up on me and tell me that I was hopeless; he explained that human beings have a barrier that protects the brain. Animals don't have this barrier and because of that, the animal testing wasn't a measure of what I could expect. He concluded that we would treat each symptom as needed, and he was certain that I would recover. So, that's what we did; the doctor came to see me every week, and treated each problem as it came up.

Living at the hotel was great, everything that I needed was quickly brought to me. I didn't have to go out for anything and I didn't want to. Going out anywhere made me extremely anxious; so anxious, that the doctor diagnosed me as having agoraphobia.

I wouldn't accept being a shut in, so I did what the doctor advised and challenged myself every day, even if I only stepped into the hallway. I kept trying, and soon I was able to go out of the room, as long as I was with Vic. Vic was very understanding and every day without fail, he took me out for a lovely lunch.

When I first started living at the hotel, Vic worked a normal shift, but later, when I began to improve, he took a side job as a bodyguard.

After Vic took on the extra job, he usually worked late into the night, and I waited up for him. Fortunately, my condition didn't affect my sexual appetite and Vic and I had wild passionate sex every night. Always intense and loud, I felt sorry for whoever was staying in the room next to us.

I spent most of my time alone, and that was fine with me, because I had a lot of work to do on myself. I didn't want to lay around and become a doorstop, so I exercised as much as I could tolerate. I ate healthy food, got plenty of rest and continued to challenge myself each day. I suffered many setbacks, but I didn't give up and it started to pay off. Gradually, I began to feel better and even got interested in painting again. Soon, the room was full of bright colorful paintings and frames. I always had a creative project to work on; I even had a sewing machine.

One day, while I was sewing, the machine jammed and stopped working. I tried everything to get it going again, but I could see that there was a broken part. I was feeling surprisingly confident that day, and decided that my challenge would be getting the sewing machine fixed. I looked in the phone book to find a sewing machine repair shop and found one on a street that I recognized. I was nervous and scared, but I knew that if I wanted to get well, I had to continue to push my boundaries, and I started off on my quest in the Porsche.

As I cautiously drove down the streets, I noticed that the same car was always behind me. I decided to find out if I was being tailed, and made a quick left. I had done enough surveillance to know that if someone was following me, they wouldn't turn directly behind me, they would go straight, come back around and then make the turn. After I made the left, the car did go straight, I made a quick U and stopped back at the intersection and watched. Sure enough, just as I had suspected, the car doubled back to come after me. There were two men, and I noted their descriptions. When they saw me sitting at the intersection, they had no choice but to go straight and I pulled out behind them and wrote down the plate number.

When the men realized that I had made them, they hit the gas to make a fast get away. My first instinct was to chase after them, but what was I going to do when I caught them? Have a shoot-out? I had the plate number, make and model of the car and the description of both men. That was enough, and I decided to head back to the hotel. I was shaken up, but no one followed me the rest of the way.

After the valet took my car, I immediately began looking for Vic and found Inky. "Hello sweetness," he greeted me.

"Inky, I've got to see Vic right away, it's important! Do you know where he is?"

"Vicious? Yeah sure, I know where he is. But is there anything that I can do to help? Are you okay?"

"I just need to see Vic."

Inky agreed to take me to where Vic was working and I followed him down a long darkened stairway, to the private rooms beneath the casino. We walked down several hallways and then through a heavy metal door. After we entered, Inky bolted it shut, "Wait here sweetness," he told me and pulled up a chair for me before he walked out of sight.

I sat down and waited, but I was anxious and started pacing. I unbolted the door and opened it, to make sure that I could escape if something went wrong, and then I closed it again. I went a ways down the hall where I had seen Inky go. I heard a door creak open, then a man screaming in pain, and when the door closed shut…silence. "Oh, a soundproof room!"

It was so quiet down there, that you could hear a pin drop. I looked around, there were no cameras, or windows; it was completely secluded. I had heard about casino's having secret rooms like this, but who would have thought that it was true?

Minutes later, I heard Vic's voice, he was infuriated, but not with me. He came huffing down the hall, pumped up and perspiring. He looked at me perplexed, why was I interrupting him while he was working?

"What's the matter baby, you feeling stressed? Did you have a panic attack? Just come ova here and let Vic hold you in his arms. Don't worry, you're gonna be just fine."

I let Vic hug me for a moment, and then told him about the two men who had followed me. He sharply pushed me away from him, "What?" he shouted. "You went out by yourself? I thought that you couldn't leave the room without me? You don't need to be going anywhere, you have everything you want! What were you doing, why were you out alone, driving on the street?" Vic was angry and on the verge of losing control.

I was frightened, I started to tremble and I slowly backed away from him. "The sewing machine broke and I just wanted to get it fixed," I said in a shaky voice.

Inky grabbed Vic by the arm, "Vic!" he said in a stern voice. "Get a grip, it's Penelope you're talking to, she's fragile."

Realizing what he had done, Vic took a breath and calmed himself down, "I'm sorry baby, after I been working, it's just hard for me to change so fast and be nice. But that's okay, there's nothing wrong with you wanting to get your sewing machine fixed. But you should have just told me about it, I would have taken care of it for ya. Now, let's all calm down and you tell me exactly what happened."

34

I explained the incident to Vic and Inky, and they decided that we should see the boss right away. The three of us were approaching his office, when who should I see, but the federal agents who had questioned me. They were exiting the office and shaking hands with the boss. On their way out they spotted me, "Well hello young lady," one of them greeted me. I was stunned and didn't answer.

"Vic, those are the FBI agents that questioned me at the jewelry store," I whispered to him.

"Yeah, I know," Vic answered, "we do them favors once in a while."

I was shocked; did the boss have the FBI in his back pocket? Had the agents been checking me out for him? Maybe the big boss wanted to find out how I would handle myself if I was ever questioned by the authorities. I quickly surmised that the whole thing had been a test and I wondered if I had passed.

Vic, Inky and I, entered the office and Vic told the boss about the two men. "I can't believe that those muthafuckas followed my ol' lady!" Vic shouted. "I ain't standin' for it!"

"Vic, everything's being taken care of, just be patient," Inky said, trying to quiet him.

"This is personal now!" Vic shouted. "I'm gonna start killin' those muthafuckas, one at a time, until I find out who done this!"

In the turmoil, I had neglected to say that I had the descriptions of the men and the license plated number. I pulled the note from my purse, "Vic here, here's the plate number and description of both of the men."

Vic took the note from my hand and glanced at it, "It sounds like Frankie Ruffalo and his idiot brother." He handed the note to the boss and then smiled at me, "I'm proud of you baby, you know how to handle yourself. I knew it the night that I met ya, when you dragged that Sheena pig across the table."

The boss looked at me approvingly, "You're cool," he said with a nod. It was only two words, but it meant that I had been accepted.

After our brief meeting with the boss, Vic took me upstairs. "I'm not working tonight, I'll be back up in a few hours, get warmed up for me," he said, and then he gave me a kiss and a squeeze and left the room.

It had been a stressful day, thoughts were racing through my mind and I was trying desperately not to have a panic attack. I decided to unwind and take a bath. I filled the tub with water and bath oil and turned on the jets.

As I slid into the warm bubbling water I tried to relax, but finding peace from the disturbing thoughts would prove to be difficult.

All that I had wanted to do was to get my sewing machine fixed, expecting that my major challenge for the day would be driving the car, but I was so wrong. Who were these men who had followed me? Apparently they were dangerous!

Seeing the Federal Agents again was no joke either; it had jolted me, and then with the added pressure of meeting the big boss, I found myself totally stressed out.

Vic was a major concern as well. Was he really going to start killing people? It was obvious what he had been doing, in the soundproof room beneath the casino. But maybe I shouldn't jump to conclusions, I could be wrong. Perhaps it just appeared as though he was working somebody over. Or was it just like the federal agents had said, Vicious Vic Valente was the enforcer!

In a gambling establishment, I would expect there to be someone with an axe to grind. When it comes to money, people get crazy. But this thing with the Ruffalos, sounded like much more than that. From what I could make of it, they were part of a crew and it all added up. There was a war going on and the enemy already had me in their sights!

I had learned from my biker friends, never to ask questions. "If someone wants you to know something, they'll tell you." I had to find out what was going on, but I knew that I couldn't start questioning Vic. Truth was, I barely knew the man and I didn't know how he would react; I had to be cautious.

While I was bathing and deep in thought, room service came in. "Just put it on the table for me please," I instructed. After they left, I got out of the tub, and as I was drying myself off, I walked out of the bathroom to see what Vic had sent up for me. Dinner was on the table, and a gift box was lying on the bed. The food smelled delicious, but I decided to open the gift first. Vic loved to see me in sexy lingerie, but he also loved to rip it off of me, so I wasn't surprised when I opened the box and found a lovely satin negligee. I slipped it on, it was pink with soft lace and ruffles and I loved it.

After I finished dinner, I reclined on the bed and waited for Vic. I was still very tense, trying to figure everything out. What was I involved in this time?

A short while later, Vic came in, he threw me a kiss and went straight to the shower. When he came out, he had one towel wrapped around his waist and was drying his hair with another, his strong muscular body glistening. "I see that you found you present," he said, and then chuckled, "actually, it was a gift to myself, I'm the one who gets the most pleasure out of it."

Vic laid on the bed beside me, "I'm sorry baby, I didn't mean to get nasty with you today. I promise that no matter what's going on with work, I'll never let it affect the way that I treat you, ever again. You're not scared, are ya? Don't let those Ruffalos shake you up, you know that I'll protect ya from anything."

Vic was truly sorry, and I figured that it was a good time for me to ask him a question, "I was wondering Vic, what's the story with these Ruffalo brothers? Why were they following me?"

"Well baby, I'll tell ya, it really ain't their fault, it's just that you're so sexy, they couldn't help theirselves. Just don't go out by yourself no more. You need anything and I'll take care of it, you already know that."

Vic slowly ran his fingers up and down the curve of my waist, admiring the beautiful gown. Then he took my hand, "Now here's something for ya," he said, and he slid a ring on my finger, a huge sparkling diamond ring!

I had been working in a jewelry store and knew that the ring was worth a fortune. Vic had said that he loved me, and now I realized that he meant it.

Before I could respond and tell him how much I loved the ring, he says, "Now all of these muthafuckas around here will see that you have a man who knows how to takes care of ya. And I'm getting rid of that Porsche too, you look like you're out on the prowl when you're driving that thin." Then Vic kissed me and slipped the soft ruffled strap, from my shoulder. He nuzzled my neck and started to growl in a low rumble, "Satisfy the beast in me baby."

Vic took a fistful of my new gown, "Vic, don't!" But it was too late, the lovely gown was already torn. Two minutes later, I didn't care about the gown, as a matter of fact, I didn't care about anything, the Feds, the Ruffalos, or the war, and least of all my car. Nothing mattered to me but my fierce hungry lion, Vicious Vic Valente. I couldn't be positive, but I thought that we might be engaged.

The next day, the doctor came to see me for our appointment. Knowing that medical records really aren't confidential, I was always careful what I told him. But as long as I didn't divulge the details, I decided that it was okay to talk about being followed in my car. "Doc, the thing that surprised me about this, is that I didn't freak out. The way that I panic over stupid things that are of no consequence, I just don't understand it."

"Well Penelope, your reaction is not unusual; panic disorder should really be called the adrenalin disease. People who suffer from panic attacks are accustomed to dealing with high levels of adrenalin on a regular basis, and in an emergency they are notoriously cool headed. When a "normal" person is flooded with adrenalin in an emergency situation, it sometimes overpowers them and they either freeze or can't think straight. That's when they can have the "panic attack.'"

I never thought that I could actually benefit from these horrible panic attacks, but it was true, I was good in emergencies. It was a comfort to know that at least I wasn't at a disadvantage when it came to emergencies. In my life, emergencies were almost the norm.

That night, Vic called the room, "I'm bringing someone up, make sure that you're dressed."

A few minutes later, Vic, came into the room with another man, "Baby, I want you to meet the man who's body I guard, this is Edwin.

Edwin was a pasty-white, sickly-looking, skinny little man, with a high whiny voice. He totally creeped me out, and when he reached out to shake my hand, I cringed, but politely greeted him. I tried to give him a firm handshake, but Edwin's hand was limp and clammy and it seemed to squish together and then slip away.

He was carrying a briefcase and after he sat down, he placed it on the coffee table.

"Go get the title for the Porsche," Vic told me.

"What do you mean? I'm not selling my car."

"I'm getting rid of that car, I told you last night."

"Vic, you know that I'll agree to anything when you're seducing me, it isn't fair, I don't want to sell my Porsche."

Edwin opened up his briefcase, it was filled to the brim with neatly-stacked, hundred dollar bills. He pulled out a stack, "Is this enough?" he asked.

Vic took me by the arm and spoke under his breath, "Baby, the car's already gone, now take the money or you get nothin'."

It was true, Vic had told me that he was getting rid of the car and I hadn't disagreed with him at the time, but I still resisted. The Porsche was my only independence. Seconds later, I realized why Vic was doing it… the Ruffalos knew the car. So I quit hesitating and quickly signed the title over to Edwin.

Edwin handed me the stack of bills, "Are you sure that it's enough?" he asked again.

"Sure, it'll be fine," I told him; I didn't even count it.

When the deal was made, Edwin closed his near-bursting briefcase and looked at Vic. "I've got a big delivery to make tomorrow night. Can you meet me at the lab?"

"Yeah sure, sure, Edwin, I'll be there at the usual time."

Both of the men left the room together, leaving me alone, and once again the brief encounter had left me with fragmented but telling facts. "Meet me at the lab?" Making deliveries? This Edwin guy looked like a mad scientist, one of those genius types from a horror movie. What legitimate laboratory makes deliveries in the cover of night? It didn't look good. Was Edwin an illegal drug manufacturer? Or was I jumping to conclusions? The tension and pressure kept pouring on me; every encounter that I had with these people created more and more suspicion. What was the truth? What was really going on?

I was plenty worried by the time Vic got home, but one look into his golden sparkling eyes and it was all over. I knew that Vic would protect me and I wasn't concerned about a thing. After all, it really wasn't any of my business anyway.

The next day, was a Saturday, and Vic told me that the boss was having a party for us that night, to celebrate our engagement. "Well, I guess I really am engaged," I concluded.

"I'll come up to get ya at about six," he said as he left the room.

"I'll be ready," I assured him.

It was a lovely evening and I decided to get ready a little early and sit outside on the patio for a while. I walked into the elevator and as I was getting off, I saw Vic standing in the lobby. He didn't see me, and I started to wave to get his attention, but then I noticed three women looking him up and down. The women were attractive and stylish; they whispered amongst themselves and then approached Vic together. I slowed my pace and waited to see what would happen next.

Strangely, the lobby was quiet enough for me to hear what was being said. The women were actually inviting Vic to come up to their room for a foursome! I was appalled! I started to rush to chase them away, but then I decided to take advantage of a rare opportunity and wait to see how Vic would handle it.

The offer seemed to take him by surprise, and he paused for a moment. I held my breath; would this be the end of my relationship? That few seconds seemed like hours, but then Vic smiled kindly and said, "That's very flattering ladies, but I'm not interested."

His statement was a relief to me, but it wasn't enough to detour these horny twisted bitches. As attractive as they were, I'm certain that they weren't accustomed to being rejected, and one of them got down on her knees and begged Vic to let her suck his cock! "Please, let me suck it, you're so hot and I can make you feel real good."

Vic grinned and then grabbed her arm, "Get up, you're embarrassing yourself," he said as he pulled her to her feet.

Vic was trying hard to gracefully get rid of these women and I quickly walked up to help. Vic noticed me approaching, "Oh, here she comes now, my beautiful fiancé," he took my hand and then kissed it. The three women called me a bitch under their breath and walked away in a huff.

"Thanks for rescuing me," Vic said, "those sure were some raunchy sluts. I think that they were about to make a scene, you really saved my ass. The boss don't like no trouble in the place."

"Yeah, I heard what they offered you, there's a lot of men that have fantasies like that."

"Not me baby, messing with those kind of pigs, I'd be afraid that my dick would fall off. Besides, I've had my share of broads. It don't mean nothin' to me, they might as well have been offering me a bologna sandwich."

I couldn't have been more pleased with Vic's comment, or with the way that he had handled the situation. I smiled sweetly at him, "Let's go, it's almost time for the party to start."

Vic and I walked hand in hand, and as we did, I thought about the pushy women. Vic was so handsome and sexy, I guess that I really couldn't blame them. They just couldn't help themselves, and either could I.

Vic and I walked into the beautifully decorated, banquet room, just as our guests were arriving. They were a loud boisterous bunch, and all seemed happy about the engagement. They made a point to make me feel appreciated and special.

We were seated at elegant tables and served an extravagant meal. The champagne flowed freely and when we were halfway through the luscious dessert, the boss stood up and proposed a toast. As we sipped our champagne, the band began to play, and an Elvis impersonator made his lavish entrance.

Elvis sang a special love song to Vic and me; it was a bit overdone, everyone was watching and I was a little embarrassed. When his song was finished, the band broke out in a wild rock and roll tune; Elvis threw me a kiss and then turned and went up on stage. He started to sing the lively song, but when he gyrated his hips, he almost fell off the stage!

"That guy's got a hard on for you," Vic said to me.

"Come on now, Vic, not everyone has a thing for me. Knock it off, don't start with this jealous crap and spoil the party."

"No, I'm not kiddin'," Vic chuckled, "look," he pointed.

Vic wasn't kidding, there was Elvis performing on stage and through his tight pants, there it was… a raging hard on!

I just laughed, "Just feel sorry for the guy Vic; it's embarrassing, give him a break."

Luckily, none of the men wanted to admit that they had noticed another man's hard on, and never said anything about it. That conversation was left to the girls, in private… yes, it was quite a show.

Later that week, Vic came up to the room and announced, "We're moving out of the hotel. Living here was fine when I was single, but now that I have you, we need a place of our own. I'm tired of these assholes always having their noses in our business."

Vic immediately went to the phone and called a realtor. He told the realtor that we wanted a secluded place, outside of the city. "I'm a busy man so don't waste my time and show me some dump. I want something extravagant, my fiancé is a super, high-class broad."

That same day, the realtor took us out toward the barren rock hills. There wasn't much built out there, but she said that she had found us the perfect place. "This house was built by a prominent physician," she told us, "it's never been lived in; as soon as the house was completed he committed suicide." She turned off of the main highway and we headed down a long road, there was nothing in sight but scrub brush for miles in all directions. Then, the realtor turned onto a long driveway that ran up the side of a hill. The house was well hidden, backed up to a high rock cliff.

Vic got out of the car and looked around, "I like the location," he said with a smile, "one road in, and you can see it for miles." Then he looked at the rock cliff, "Yeah, I like it alright, no muthafucka could scale that cliff and get away from me. You sneak a man in here, and he's a dead man walking."

Vic's comment threw me; did he think that I was cheating on him? Is that why we were moving? No … he had to be kidding!

We went inside, and the house was stunning, spacious rooms and all of the modern conveniences. There was a huge swimming pool and spa on the edge of the cliff overlooking the desert. It was a magnificent home and I was excited, "I like living at the hotel, Vic, but you're right, we need a place of our own. I love this house."

"Now you sure you want this one baby? You don't want to see something else before you make up your mind?"

"Yes, I'm sure, let's get it."

"You made yourself a deal lady, now how much is it?" Vic asked as he pulled a wad of cash from his pocket.

Vic handled everything concerning the move, he wouldn't let me lift a finger to help. "You don't work for me," he said, "all I expect from you is to love me." So, I waited at the hotel for everything to be ready.

Fortunately, it didn't take long. The crew worked fast and the house was finished in no time. Vic came to get me and when we pulled up through the gate, I saw a new Cadillac parked in the driveway. Vic handed me the keys, "Here you go baby, there's your new car. You'll look like you belong to somebody when you're driving that thing."

I was ecstatic; just moving into the luxurious home was exciting enough, but now I had a new Cadillac too! I gave Vic a big kiss and thanked him for the car, then we entered the house together. Everything was sparkling clean and brightly polished, with colorful fresh flowers in every room. All of the dishes were put away, the freezer and refrigerator stocked, beds made, and even my clothes were neatly in the closet. "Yeah, they done a good job," Vic commented.

"Yes they certainly did," I agreed.

"Are ya happy baby? That's all that I want is for you to be happy." Vic picked me up and we went to the bedroom. Things couldn't have been any better.

The next day, Vic had a sophisticated security system installed, and then he built a safe room. The safe room was sound and bullet proof, it was stocked with survival supplies and had a wall of shelves filled with weapons and ammunition. Maybe I was crazy, but it didn't concern me; as a matter of fact, it made me feel safe.

I enjoyed living in the lovely home; being away from the casino proved to be good for me, and soon I was strong enough to take a walk every day.

One morning, while I was walking, a German Shepherd came running up to me, he seemed distressed, but wasn't injured. The dog was panting heavily and very thirsty, so I took him home and gave him water and a nice steak. After that, I loaded him up in the car and drove toward the highway looking for his owner. There was a truck parked at the turnoff, and when the driver saw the dog, he jumped out and ran up to my car. I immediately released the dog and the two of them had a happy boisterous reunion. The man was tearing up, he was so happy to find his cherished pet. He told me that the dog had fallen out of the back of the truck and that he wasn't sure exactly where it had happened.

He explained that he was on his way to hike at a nature trail, and invited me to come along. I was interested to find out where the nature trail was; it was already getting boring walking down the driveway and looking at nothing but scrub brush, so I followed him in my car.

The trail wasn't far down the highway, and was a scenic hike. I thought that I would enjoy it, but I had already walked enough for the day and I was tired. I thanked the man and started home, looking forward to walking on the trail the next morning.

When I pulled up to the house, Vic was there; I was surprised to find him home so early in the day. I walked in the door and gave him a hug and kiss hello and then explained how I had found a German Shepherd and returned it to its' owner. "The owner was a very nice man," I went on to say, "he showed me a nature trail and I plan to go there tomorrow morning for a hike."

I thought that Vic would be happy that I was feeling well enough to start hiking, but he was furious and accused me of cheating on him. I couldn't believe it! All that he had heard was that a *man* had shown me where the trails were.

"He probably seen you walkin' and sent the dog after ya! I know how these muthafuckas think, he planned the whole thing, he wants you. He could have raped you or anything!"

"Vic calm down, nothing happened, he just showed me where the trail was. What's really going on here? Is it the Ruffalos, is that what you're worried about?"

"No, no, it ain't the Ruffalos we've reached an understanding. Then Vic tried to regain his composure, "I'm sorry baby," he said calmly, "I'm just spoiled and used to having you home, and when I come back today, I missed ya and I wanted ya, but you weren't here. Then you tell me that you were with some strange man! I'm telling ya baby, you got to be more careful! These assholes I deal with… you can't trust nobody, you never know who they might be. You could get kidnapped or hurt real bad. Now promise me, you won't go nowheres by yourself no more."

"Okay, okay," I agreed.

"Now I realize that you're feeling better and you want to go places, but I don't like you going anywheres by yourself. It's too dangerous and I don't want you, never, ever, on that trail!"

"Okay, okay."

"But don't worry, I know how you broads are, you need to go shoppin' and talk to each other, once in a while; you know, about woman stuff. Wouldn't you rather go out and spend money and buy yourself some nice things? Doesn't that sound better than walking out in the dirt? I know you need a friend, and I'll send one over for ya, but I got to go to work now." Vic kissed me good-bye and then he left.

I knew that Vic wasn't freaking out about nothing; there was always a reason for everything he said and did. I didn't know what was going on this time, but I did know that no matter how much I tried to have a normal life with Vic, it was clear that things could never be that way.

A few hours later, as I was finishing lunch and the stupid alarm went off… WHOAAAOOO … WHOAAAOOO …WHOAAAOOO!!!!! The ear piercing noise was blasting through my brain. "Are they ever going to get that damn alarm fixed?!" I shouted angrily as I walked to the keypad. With all of the money that Vic had spent on the sophisticated alarm system, it never worked right; and so far none of the technicians had been able to repair it correctly. As soon as they had one problem fixed, something else would go wrong. I was fed up, cussing and punching in the code, over and over again, trying to get it to stop, when I noticed someone at the gate. When the alarm finally turned off, I hit the intercom, "Who's there?" I asked,

"It's Wendy, Vic sent me over to take you shopping. I know where all the good stores are."

I remembered what Vic had said earlier and guessed that Wendy must be my "friend." I chuckled as I hit the remote and opened the gate.

I walked out of the house and introduced myself to Wendy. She was about my age, tough looking and a bit overweight, but still attractive. She told me that Vic had given her money for us to shop.

Wendy seemed nice enough, but when I started to get into my Cadillac, she stopped me, "No, Vic wants us to take my car." I agreed, and the two of us rode off on our day of shopping. I wondered how much Vic was paying her to be my "friend."

Wendy was the talkative type and she told me all about herself. She said that she had a daughter and unashamedly admitted that she had been having sex with three different men at the time that she got pregnant. Wendy wasn't sure who the father was, but the interesting part was that all three of these men wanted to be the parent, and none of them would agree to a paternity test. They all paid child support, and the little girl called each of them different versions of daddy. I don't know how anyone else would interpret such a situation, but personally, I believed that Wendy must have been a special woman to elicit such devotion.

Wendy told me that she worked for Vic as his assistant. "Yeah, Vic likes me around, I watch his back and take good care of him. That's why he sent me today, to kinda take care of you too," she told me.

"Yeah sure," I thought, "more like, babysit me."

Wendy freely divulged information, and she knew everything about everybody, so I decided to take advantage and find out a few things. "I haven't seen Thumbs around lately," I commented.

"Oh, haven't you heard? The D. A. wouldn't make the deal, the trial's been going on for two weeks now."

"Oh yeah, what was the charge again?"

"He worked some guy over for Vinnie and popped his eyeball out. They're making a big deal out of it and it looks he'll end up doing some time. The damn prosecutor is bringing in the bloody clothes as evidence to show how severe the beating was. Thumbs' attorney tried to get it excluded but he couldn't, it happens to him every time! Poor Thumbs, he gets so pissed off."

"You know, Wendy, it only takes four and a half pounds of pressure to pop out an eyeball, maybe Thumbs didn't mean to do it."

"Sorry Penelope, this ain't the first time. Why do you think they call him Thumbs?"

The news was shocking, but I didn't miss a beat. "Oh, and while we're on the subject, why do they call Inky, Inky? Is he in the printing business?"

"You mean like counterfeiting?"

"Okay…Yeah sure."

"No, he's called Inky because he robbed a bank. He made it out and even switched to another vehicle. The fool was home free, driving down the street out of town, when he sees a cop car. Instead of turning the other way, the smart ass pulls up right along-side and waves. Yeah, he was cool alright, he's ice cubes, he thinks, got the cash right on the seat next to him, then the ink pack blows, right in front of the cops. They caught him of course, and he was stained with ink for, I don't know how long."

Wendy started laughing, and I laughed right along with her, but it wasn't at all humorous to me. "That's pretty funny alright," I played along. "I would have never thought that Inky would do something like that, he's such a sweet old man and he seems so honest," I commented.

"Yeah, you wouldn't know it now, but Inky used to be a real asshole. He's totally different now, reformed I guess. It's no act either, he really is a great guy." Wendy paused for a moment in thought, and then went on; "Yeah, Inky's a true friend alright, I really trust him. He's pulled my bacon out of the fire on more than one occasion. Inky keeps the guys in line, he knows what he's talking about and they respect him for it. Yep, things would go downhill pretty fast without the Wise Old Owl."

I remembered how Inky had intervened between Vic and me, when Vic was scaring me in the casino basement. "Yeah you're right about that Wendy, even Vic listens to him."

"Oh yeah, they all listen to Inky, he's got their best interest at heart and they know it; he's kinda like a father."

I was glad to hear that Inky was a standup guy. I was very fond of him and held him in high regard. It was nice to know that my trust hadn't been misguided. But then, I quickly went on to ask Wendy more questions. "What about Digger? What's his nickname about?"

"Now Digger is another smart-ass. He whacks some guy, and instead of taking the body out to the desert to bury, the lazy son-of-a-bitch decides to dig a hole in this "field" he finds where the ground is soft. The next day… it's all over the news, body found buried in Judge Milburn's private golf course. Unbelievable ain't it?"

"Yeah, unbelievable Wendy, and I'm not even going to ask you about The Ratchet."

The stories that I had heard were unbelievable all right, but horribly fearfully true. I didn't want to hear anymore, but Wendy kept on talking, even while we went from store to store spending Vic's money. I had to act like the things that she was telling me were no big deal, but after a while my head was buzzing and I was feeling very anxious. I had to have the time to pull myself together before I saw Vic that night, so I made up an excuse. "Wendy, I have a terrible headache," I told her, "would you mind cutting it short today?"

I couldn't wait to get home, and as soon as I did, Wendy and I quickly exchanged phone numbers and I sent her away.

After she was gone, I laid on the bed and tried to relax. The things that Wendy had told me really shouldn't have been such a shock to me, but they were. Knowing the details didn't change anything; it was just that I couldn't live in denial any longer.

That night, when Vic came home, he was excited to hear how my day had gone with Wendy. "Did you girls have a nice time?" he asked. "Wendy's great ain't she?"

"Yes she is," I agreed, "I really liked her and we did have a nice time together."

"Let me see what you bought," Vic said smiling.

As I pulled things from the shopping bags, Vic insisted that I model them for him. He whistled and made a big deal as I walked down the staircase in each new outfit. He was always happy when he had made me happy.

After the fashion show was done, and I had changed back into my jeans, I felt much better, and decided to make Vic his favorite dinner, fried chicken. He especially liked drumsticks, and I had a whole package of them. I had opened the chicken and begun to prepare it when I found that the drumsticks were limp, all of the bones had been broken. "Vic," I said, "something's wrong with these chicken legs, all of the bones are broken. Maybe I shouldn't fix them."

"Forget about it baby, I just like to keep in practice," he chuckled.

I made a flippant remark, as if to go along with the joke, but strangely, it upset me more than anything else I had heard that day. It was obvious that Vic enjoyed breaking bones.

As he lay next to me in bed that night, I wondered why they called him Vicious. I was sure that there was good reason for it. Nicknames were always earned and I didn't ever want to know what he had done to deserve it; no more than I wanted to know how Chainsaw Charlie had gotten his name. I was desperately in love with Vic, he cherished and cared for me and he knew how to love me. Vic had been there for me when I needed him and I was going try my best to work things out. After all, what would I do without him?

Days later, when the time was right, I gathered my courage and sat Vic down. I told him that if we were going to stay together he had to make the break from his associates. I didn't know how he would react to such a demand, and was both pleased and surprised when I found no resistance.

"Baby, I know you're right, but it's almost impossible for me to find a job, nobody will hire a convicted felon. The only thing that I can do is start my own business, but I'll need a lot of cash to get up and running. Just give me some time to get enough money together and then I'll get out. Be patient, and baby I promise, everything will be fine."

I prayed that Vic would be able to make the break.

Months went by, and everything remained status quo, Vic went to work every day, the alarm system continued to malfunction, and I occasionally spent time with Wendy. I wasn't expecting a miracle, but I was hoping to see some progress very soon.

It was about three o' clock one afternoon, Vic had just left and I was baking cookies, when I heard someone at the gate. I hit the intercom; it was Edwin, "I just saw Vic on the road, he's coming back in ten minutes to meet with me, and he wants me to wait for him here."

I hesitated for a moment, it didn't sound like Vic; he would never want me to be alone with another man. But Vic worked for Edwin, and I didn't want to offend him, so I opened the gate and then invited him into the house. "Come on in Edwin," I said in a friendly tone. "I'm baking chocolate chip cookies, why don't you join me in the kitchen."

I led Edwin through the living room, to the back of the house and seated him at the table, rather than on the sofa. I wanted to keep him as far away from me as possible and I felt more comfortable with the large kitchen table between us.

"Would you like to try some of my cookies?" I asked. "The first batch will be done in two minutes."

Edwin sat down, "Oh yes, I'd like to try a cookie," he said in his shrill voice.

"Why don't we have a glass of milk," I suggested, "nothing like milk and cookies." I poured the milk and served the cookies, then I sat down across the table from Edwin, "the creepy mad scientist."

Edwin had on a pair of gloves. "Edwin would you like me to take your gloves? It'll be kinda hard dunking your cookies with them on?"

"No, no thank you, I have to keep them on," he said anxiously. "You see, I have a seeping rash on my hands," then he hesitated, "it's… it's from a chemical burn."

"Oh I'm sorry to hear that," I told him, praying that Vic would hurry home. Eeewww, could this guy get any grosser?

"These cookies have a very unique texture and flavor," Edwin commented.

"Yes, I use whole wheat flour and put in twice as much as the recipe calls for, then I add an extra egg. The cookies have more body that way and they're not as sweet."

"Very interesting," Edwin said as he closely examined the cookie. "Baking is a science and it appears that you have achieved the right formula, very delicious. This milk is good too, not what I'm used to drinking."

"Yes, it's raw milk. I was raised milking cows, can't bring myself to drink processed milk."

"Very interesting," Edwin said again. "You must know pertinent information about cows that others can't read about in books. What are cows like, what kind of nature do they have?"

I explained all about cows to Edwin. I told him how I used to watch them graze with my horse, Dynamite, when I was a kid. And about Moo Moo, how she would wrap her neck around me to warm me up when it was cold and windy. "Cows are actually very sweet animals; I love cows,

49

but keep clear of the bulls. A bull will knock you down and grind you into the ground with his horns, until there's nothing left of you. You can't trust a bull, they're very dangerous animals."

"Males do tend to be more aggressive than females," Edwin said, "it's the testosterone. And now I'd like to change the subject, if you don't mind. You seem like a knowledgeable person and I have another question for you," then Edwin calmly pulled a small gun from his jacket.

This Edwin guy was a first-class weirdo and I was concerned about him pulling out a gun, but I didn't let on. "Nice little gun," I commented. "Is that a .25 Beretta; the one with the tip up barrel? I'd like to have one myself."

"Yes it is," Edwin answered, "and according to my sources, if someone is shot in the head with a small caliber gun, such as this one, the bullet will bounce around inside the skull and will mean a sure kill, rather than a bigger gun that will pass through the brain and give the person a chance of survival. Do you know if my facts are correct?"

"Uh…yeah, it's true."

"I'm glad to know that my information is accurate," Edwin happily exclaimed. This gun is a very special gun, it has Vic's fingerprints on it."

Vic's fingerprints on the gun, this couldn't be a good sign. Something was up and I knew that things were about to take a dangerous turn. "Oh Edwin, is that Vic's gun?" I asked trying to remain calm.

"No Penelope, it's my gun, but ironically Vic's the one who showed me how to use it. It's important to me that you know that you haven't made this easy for me; I find you strangely appealing, but I won't let that stop me from doing what I must." Edwin's eyes turned dark and he pointed the gun at my face, "Penelope, I'm going to frame Vic for a murder today …. your murder!"

I shuddered, this creep was planning to shoot me in the head! My first thought was to try and knock the gun from his hand, but sitting across the table, he was just too far away. I realized that my best chance was to try to talk him out of it. "Now Edwin, why would you want to do a thing like that?" I asked, hoping that he would answer me and not just pull the trigger.

I considered myself lucky when Edwin decided to talk, "Vic is going to suffer for what he's done to me. He took my business and forces me to work for *him* now! He took everything from me! I have nothing!"

Edwin's hands were shaking and I was fearful that he might shoot me accidentally; I could only hope that the gun didn't have a hair trigger. He went on talking and slurping saliva back into his mouth. "The only thing that's important to Vic is you, and what better way for me to achieve my revenge than to have him serving a life sentence for the murder of his beloved, Penelope. He will sit rotting in a cell in agony, without his true love!"

"Wow Edwin, that sounds like an excellent revenge plan, very well thought out," I said, while I quivered inside. "You've got his fingerprints and everything, all you have to do is shoot me, drop the gun and get out before for the police to show up." Then I paused, "On second thought, I guess that you'll have to call the police yourself, if Vic comes home and finds me dead, he'll get rid of the evidence before the police ever find out. And then he'll come looking for you! You wouldn't want that to happen, we both know how vicious he can be."

"Oh no, I wouldn't want that!" Edwin agreed and then began to tremble. The thought of Vic coming after him was more than he could handle.

"Edwin, Edwin, listen to me, I'm going to tell you a secret."

Edwin looked at me questioning, "A secret?"

"Yes a secret about Vic and me, would you like to hear it?"

"Oh yes, I would."

"I hate Vic; I hate him even more than you do. Vic isn't nice to me; he treats me like a slave. I'm his prisoner and he makes me do all kinds of unspeakable things. He's very happy, but I'm miserable and I feel like I'm living in hell."

Edwin seemed pleased at the revelation that Vic's beloved Penelope hated him, and he smiled.

I went on, "I could never love a brutish man like Vic, I might as well try to fall in love with an ape, he's so primitive and stupid. Vic just forced himself into my life; he wanted me and he didn't even care what I thought about it.

"He certainly is brutish," Edwin agreed.

"A man like that has never appealed to me; I like a more sensitive intelligent man, someone like you, for instance. I liked you from the first time we met, Edwin, when you bought my car. I've been waiting all this time to tell you how I feel. Why do you think I invited you in the house so quickly? Vic has tried everything to keep me away from you." I smiled, hoping that Edwin would take the bait and lower the gun, but he was too smart and didn't falter, so I sweetened the pot.

"Edwin, how bout the two of us put our heads together and devise a plan? I can get my hands on a lot of big money. Vic has millions in cash stashed away from his other interests. It would be easy for me to take it and we would be set for life.

This plan seemed to appeal to Edwin.

I was making progress and getting through to him. The only thing that could blow it now, was if Vic came home and interrupted. I knew that Edwin would shoot him the minute he walked through the door.

I had to work fast; Edwin was hooked, but now I needed to reel him in. "Do you like the tropics?" I asked. "Wouldn't it be nice to get away from here, away from all of our problems? Erase all of the bad memories and create new ones of our own? We could take a picture of the two of us sitting on the beach together and send it to Vic. That would kill him; seeing another man with his hands on me would be worse for him than if I were dead. You taking the money and stealing his girl, the ultimate revenge. Vic doesn't mind prison you know, they treat him like a big shot in there."

Edwin was agreeing with me and he stopped shaking. I knew that it would be only minutes before I could make my move, when... WHOAAAOOO ... WHOAAAOOO ...WHOAAAOOO... WHOAAAOOO!!!!! The damn alarm went off! Vic was home!

Edwin flinched, and immediately I lunged across the table and grabbed the gun. I tried to pull it from his grasp, but his glove bunched up in the trigger guard and the gun started firing bullets into the ceiling and walls.

Vic ran into the room where Edwin and I were wrestling for the gun. "Vic get out, now! There's three more rounds!" I screamed above the ear-piercing alarm.

Vic didn't listen to me, and in a split second he had Edwin on his knees with his face to the floor. "What the fuck are you doing with this guy?" he angrily asked.

I stood up, "Fighting for the gun! I warned you not to come in, you could have been shot!"

Vic wasn't amused, "Baby I told you... never let any of these muthafuckas in the house! These people that I do business with are dangerous.... Or maybe you want this guy? Is that why you let him in?

Is that what you like, the brainy type?"

Then Vic addressed Edwin, "You come here thinkin' that you're gonna fuck my ol' lady? Is that what you did, you muthafucka?"

Vic tightened his grip on Edwin, "Please Vic don't shoot me," he begged.

"Shoot you?! You think I need a gun to handle you, you fuckin' pussy?! Vic picked Edwin up and threw him across the room. He slammed against the wall and then collapsed on the floor.

"You see baby, what happens when you don't listen to me?" Vic shouted above the sounding alarm. "Now I've got to take care of this situation. You see what you done?"

Vic walked toward Edwin and picked him up again. "Did you want to see me beat the shit out of him? Maybe that's what you wanted when you let this fucka in my house. Here watch me break his arm. Does this turn you on?" Vic twisted Edwin's arm and even above the alarm, I heard the crack as the bone broke.

Edwin was screaming and crying. "SHUT UP!" Vic shouted as he threw him across the room again.

My guilt mounted, Vic was right, I knew better than to let Edwin in the house. What had I done? I stood there in shock as the unrelenting alarm pierced my ears and Vic pounded Edwin with his mallet-like fists. I watched the blood splatter on the walls and run down to the floor. I wondered how much blood the human body held as the room turned more and more crimson.

Vic stopped the beating for a moment, "Baby, turn off that damn alarm!"

I went to the keypad and punched in the code, my hands were shaking as I tried unsuccessfully, again and again, to stop the alarm from wailing.

"Come on baby; get that fuckin' alarm turned off!" Vic shouted above the maddening noise.

"I'm trying Vic! I just can't get it!"

Vic grabbed Edwin and dragged him across the room toward me.

"That's okay baby," Vic said kindly, "you're just nervous, here let me do it." I backed away, fearfully keeping my eyes on Vic, while he punched in the code. I didn't know how much more it would take before he turned his anger towards me. When the alarm didn't stop the first time, Vic hit the wall and knocked a hole in it. "I pay top dollar for a state of the art security system and this is what I get!"

"Vic just try it again, it might work this time," I shouted hopefully.

Vic punched in the code one more time, and finally the alarm was quieted. "There baby, now isn't that better? You be sure to call and have that alarm fixed in the morning. Tell them that if they can't do it right this time, they can just take the whole thing out."

"Okay," I calmly agreed, but I was terrified. How would this all end?

Vic noticed that Edwin was bleeding in the entryway. "Great, we got blood in here too, now Vinnie's gonna charge me for an extra room!" Vic was disgusted as he dragged Edwin back into the family room. I followed behind him, afraid that he was going to kill Edwin, but then suddenly, I realized that I was more afraid if Vic didn't kill him. I didn't know what I should do, so I just stood there. I couldn't think straight.

Vic dropped Edwin on the floor and gave him a kick; it reminded me of a cat playing with a mouse, batting it around until it didn't move anymore. "I guess he's had enough," he laughed.

Vic picked Edwin up and threw him one more time. He landed on the recliner and it slowly eased back. Edwin laid there, motionless, and I felt a morbid gloom. Surely he must be dead.

Vic noticed me standing there shaking, "Baby, you look scared. You're not afraid of me, are you?" He reached for me with his bloody hands and pulled me close to him. "Don't be afraid, I would never hurt you, I love you baby," he said and then he started to kiss me.

I didn't want to kiss Vic; it was true, I was scared of him, but I didn't resist. "You just have to learn to listen to me. You see what happens when you don't listen?" he said in a mild tone.

Vic ran his hands up and down my body. "You've got a great ass baby," he said, breathing heavily, and then he unzipped my jeans. I backed away from him, but he wouldn't let me go, he just pressed toward me and when I hit the sofa he pushed me down on it. Vic got on top of me, ripped open my shirt and began to kiss my breasts. I looked over at Edwin's limp bloody body lying in the chair and I couldn't stand it. I started to get up, but Vic grabbed my jeans and forced me down as he pulled them off of me.

I looked around and saw Edwin's blood slowly moving, as if crawling down the walls of the room. It seemed as though it was alive and screaming out to me. Blood was smeared on my stomach and legs and it was in my hair. I couldn't cope, I felt like the whole thing wasn't really happening.

Vic was determined to have his way, so I closed my eyes and made the best of it. I don't know if it was the violence or the blood that turned Vic on, but he was more passionate than ever and I started to enjoy the intense sex. My heart was racing, I was panting and perspiring, I had forgotten about everything and was lost in pure abandon, but just as I reached the peak, I turned my head and inadvertently looked at Edwin. His face was covered with deep dark-red blood and suddenly, he opened his eyes and looked right at me! His eyes seemed to jump out like bright-white, horrifying hell fire!

It jolted me, "Vic! He's looking at me!" I screamed.

"That's okay, let the muthafucka watch, he ain't going nowhere."

All of the terror and violence, all of the blood and fear, I felt a release from it all as Vic and I went over the top, like we had never done before. When it was over, we both laid there, breathing hard and holding each other tight.

I slowly came down from the unfathomable high and felt grim reality closing in. Vic was still beside me when the phone started to ring and he picked it up, "It's the security company," he told me. "Yes, yes, it's me, everything's fine here." Then he stopped and looked around at the blood drenched walls surrounding us and said the code word... RED. It sent a shiver down my spine.

Vic got up and walked to the refrigerator to get a drink, and I wondered, "What should my next move be?" I noticed the little Beretta on the floor by the sofa; I picked it up and laid there with crazy thoughts racing through my mind. Before I could sort them out, Vic took my hand and gently sat me up, "Come on baby, you're going upstairs and get some rest." I was wearing nothing but my torn shirt. Vic took it off of me and then picked me up; he carried me across the blood splattered floor and put me down on the first step of the staircase.

"Vic what are we going to do?" I asked.

"We ... aren't going to do anything, I can handle this. Now just go on upstairs and relax, keep the gun if you want to. And don't come back down!"

I nodded my head in reply and turned to climb the stairs. Vic gave me a pat on the fanny, "Like I said, great ass baby." He smiled, and then went to make a phone call.

When I reached the first landing, I started to shake. "What was going to happen? Were we going to prison? I stopped and leaned against the wall. I could hear Vic talking on the phone, "Hey Vinnie, I've got a situation here. How soon can you be at my place?"

A moment later, he called Wendy. "I need you at the house, and swing by Vito's on the way, he's holding something for me; pick it up." After Vic hung up, he started moving things around.

I had been working hard for months, struggling to recover from the carbon monoxide poisoning. I was just starting to get my strength back, and now, it had all been used up. It wasn't just looking down the barrel of a gun, or the horror of watching Vic beat Edwin. It was my relationship with Vic; now there was no doubt, being with him was dangerous. Another relationship... another big problem, it was a bitter disappointment. I loved Vic, but it would take more than his sparkling eyes and hot body to erase all of my cares away this time.

I raised my eyes and looked at the long stairway; it seemed like a high mountain and I wondered how I would ever climb it. One step at a time, I struggled and pulled myself up with the railing. When I reached the top, I went into the bathroom and showered, but I didn't have the strength to dry myself off, so I threw a towel down on my pillow and climbed into bed.

I lay there listening. I could hear people coming in and out of the house, things were being dragged and banged around and water was running.

I smelled a fire, and remembered that horrible day when, Pat, and I had burned our clothes after our hostile confrontation with Larry. I never thought that I would ever be in another dreadful situation like that again, but here I was, my clothes were being burned, just like before when someone had wanted to destroy me.

"How did I get myself into these situations? Why is it that these things happened to me?" Soon I realized that there were no real answers to my questions and I decided to consider myself lucky; I was the one who had survived, yet again.

It was late, Vic and the crew were finished cleaning things up, and I heard them all leave. Vic came up to the room and climbed into bed with me. He wrapped his arms around me, "Everything's been taken care of, now let's get some sleep."

"Is Edwin dead?" I asked.

"No, no, he's not dead; if I had wanted to kill him, I would have finished him off right away. I just had to teach that muthafucka a lesson, one that he won't ever forget. I wouldn't kill him, I need him to work. Wendy took the prick to the doctor. He'll be fine in a few weeks."

"What if he calls the police? Maybe we should get out of here!"

"After you kick a muthafucka's ass like that, they never call the police. Now forget about it, and please baby, go to sleep."

I was so tense that I didn't want Vic touching me, but he kept holding me and soon, I fell asleep from pure exhaustion. I woke up a few hours later with the horror of what had happened playing over and over in my mind. I felt panicky and my body was trembling. I had seen firsthand, just how vicious, Vicious Vic really was and I was deathly afraid of him. I had let Edwin into the house, and I didn't know if Vic was still angry at me because of it. I was dreading what he might do to me if he was. My adrenalin was pumping and I needed to get up; I was having a panic attack; but I couldn't move as Vic had his arms wrapped tightly around me. I laid in the dark for hours, completely possessed by fear.

When the sun came up, Vic released me and rolled over on his back. I didn't want to wake him, so I carefully pulled back the covers and slowly slipped out of bed. But when I took a few steps, I heard Vic chuckle; he was awake! I didn't look back at him, I kept walking; trying to act like everything was normal and I noticed a velvet jewelry box on my vanity. I opened the box and found a magnificent diamond and ruby choker with earrings to match. The rubies were pigeons'-blood red, and the diamonds had excellent color and clarity. I was completely stunned.

"Why don't you try them on?" Vic kindly suggested.

At that moment, I wasn't happy or afraid; it was as though I had lost the ability to feel all emotion. But I did as Vic asked, and like a robot, I put on the jewelry.

"Come ova here and let me get a closer look at you." Vic demanded.

I slowly walked back to the bed and when I was close enough, Vic pulled me down beside him.

"I got rubies because I love you in bright red lipstick," he told me. "I thought that rubies would look gorgeous on you, and I was right. I was going to wait until Christmas to give them to ya, but after what happened yesterday, it seemed like the best thing to give them to ya today. How'd I do baby, you feeling better now?"

Vic was smiling and I found his voice soothing. At that point, I knew that I wasn't facing his wrath and I began to calm down.

"Yes Vic, you did great," I answered. "These are the most exquisite jewels that I have ever seen. I love them!"

"I just want you to be happy baby," Vic said as he laid close beside me. He gently traced the outline of my lips with his sturdy finger, and then admired one of the sparkling earrings, dangling from my ear. "When I fall in love, I fall all the way, and there ain't nothing that I won't do for ya." He reached behind my neck and took hold of the choker, pulling it snugly around my throat, "You can never leave me," he said, looking deep into my eyes. Then Vic released the choker, and kissed me passionately. He pulled my leg across him and sat me up on top of him, "Now I got something else for ya baby," he said as he eased me down on his hard piece of steel. "Now, I want to watch you while you're loving me, you're so beautiful."

As Vic and I made love, my emotions returned and I found that I still loved him. After all, he really hadn't done anything wrong. It wasn't his fault that Edwin had tried to shoot me; all Vic had done was protect me. I decided to put the past behind and hope for the best.

For weeks after the encounter with Edwin, Vic was extremely busy and it was near impossible for me to talk to him about anything. So, I decided to call Wendy and go on another shopping trip to find out what had really happened to Edwin. Did we have a murder charge hanging over our heads?

Wendy confirmed that Edwin was still alive, "He's got his jaw wired shut; it was busted in two places, his nose is broken and he has a cast on his arm. Vic sure beat the shit out of him and the boys say that he did us all a favor; Edwin has a much better attitude now. I guess that everyone needs their ass kicked at least once in their lives, you know, a little attitude adjustment. You can always tell when some smart-ass has never had his ass kicked."

I thought about what Wendy had said, and she was absolutely right, you can tell when some smart-ass has never had a good ass-whuppin'.

I had found out what I wanted to know; Edwin wasn't dead and it sounded like he was under control and wouldn't be bothering me again. But was Wendy merely telling me what Vic had instructed her to?

Wendy and I were headed home when we saw a trail of smoke billowing in the sky. "That smoke's coming from Inky's place!" Wendy shouted. She slammed on the brakes and quickly turned the car around. I could hear the sirens wailing as Wendy pressed to get to the scene ahead of them. When we pulled up to Inky's house, Vic's car was ablaze. I was terrified; had Vic been killed in the explosion? Wendy and I frantically jumped out of the car just as Vic came bursting out of Inky's house. He was holding a bloody kitchen towel over one eye and carrying a big black suitcase. "Wendy open your trunk!" he shouted to her. Then he noticed me, "What the hell is she doing here?"

"I'm sorry Vic," Wendy apologized, "we were in the area and I came straight over."

"I don't care if you've been shot in the head, you take Penelope home before you go to the hospital! You know better than to bring her around any of this shit! Now she's seen it, and I'm going to have to deal with her!"

"I know, I'm sorry man."

"Now get the damn trunk open and get this suitcase out of here before the fuckin' cops show up!"

While Vic was screaming at Wendy, I saw Inky lying on the lawn. He was badly hurt and I ran to try and help him. When I got closer, I found that he was conscious and I knelt down beside him.

"Everything's going to be okay, sweetness," Inky whispered as he winced in pain. "Don't give up on Vic, he's a good boy, he just lacks direction."

Vic shouted to me from across the lawn, "Come on baby, let's get out of here!"

"But Inky, he's hurt! I can't leave him!"

"Baby, I dragged him out of the car and called the ambulance. What more do you want me to do? Now come on!"

Inky's body jerked. "Inky!!" I said, "hold on, the ambulance is almost here!"

Inky was coughing and blood was running from his mouth, "Tell Vic that it was the…"

"Inky, don't try to talk, just hold on!"

Inky grabbed my sleeve and said, "Ruffalos," then his body went limp and he was dead! I didn't cry, I didn't move, I just sat there helplessly looking at my sweet dead friend.

Vic ran over and took my hand, "Come on, we're leaving!" he shouted as he pulled me up and dragged me across the yard. There was nothing that I could do for Inky, and a part of me went numb, but crossing the yard, I suddenly became terrified. I felt like I was walking in a minefield, fearful of what would blow up next. Vic opened the door to Inky's car and started to push me inside. "Vic, this car might blow up too! I'll just walk! Let me go!" I struggled to get away from him.

The car ain't gonna blow up! I already looked it ova! Now shut up and get inside!" I quit fighting and let Vic push me in, he started the motor and raced away. "Baby, you got to learn to listen to me!" Vic said sternly, shaking his head.

I started to cry, "Poor Inky," I sobbed, "he's dead!"

Vic and I sat in silence the rest of the way home, and once we were inside the house, he got in the shower, still without speaking a word to me.

I was concerned about his head injury, but when I tried to look at it, he protested. Blood was running down the shower drain as we argued. "Vic, we better call the doctor, you need stitches!"

"I ain't calling Lenny! Now quit nagging me!"

"But you're bleeding badly."

"It's a head injury, what do you expect?" Vic got out of the shower and went to the mirror, blotting the wound with a towel.

"Let me see," I said, reaching for him. "It looks like it's beginning to clot."

"Get the fuck away from me, it ain't nothing!" he barked as he pushed me away.

When Vic pushed me, I snapped, "It ain't nothing! It ain't nothing! Inky's dead, and all you have to say is, 'It ain't nothing!' Inky told me that it was the Ruffalos. You said that you had an understanding with them and that they wouldn't give us any more trouble, and now Inky's dead! Tell me the truth Vic, what's going on? I told you to break away from these guys, but you wouldn't listen to me, and now things are even worse than before!"

"The Ruffalos?! Inky told you that it was the Ruffalos?! I should have whacked those muthafuckas right out the gate, but I was trying to be a nice guy. Well no more, I'm going to slaughter every one of 'em!"

"What the hell are you doing Vic? Let's just move away from here, I don't want to worry about you every time you leave the house! I can't take it anymore!"

"You can't take it?!" Vic screamed back at me. "You're the one that can't take it anymore? Tell me what's so difficult about your life! You've got people that take care of everything around here, the pool, the garden, and Rosita to cook and clean the house. When you said that you wanted to exercise, I set up a gym for ya. And what about that fancy doctor? Let me tell ya baby, that guy ain't cheap. And who bought ya the rock you're wearing on your finger, and the brand new Cadillac? You live in a big beautiful home, and this ain't just any house, you wanted the most expensive house that the damn realtor could find! This stuff don't come easy baby and I have to pay cash for everything, I can't get no credit, so I do what I gotta do."

Vic walked over to the closet, he opened the door and stepped inside. "Tell me, what's so difficult about your life again? Maybe I'm missing something." He pulled out my white ermine fur and threw it on the bed. "What about this coat and all your designer clothes? Maybe it's the Italian leather boots and the shoes and pocketbooks that make your life so difficult!"

Vic was in a fury, throwing my clothes out of the closet and shouting. Then suddenly, he stopped, "What about me? Every time I come home and you aren't here, I'm afraid that you've left me! I done everything for ya! What the hell more do you expect from me? All I want is for you to be happy. I would have taken you on exotic vacations, but you don't want to go nowhere. What else can I do? You got everything in the world, but are ya happy? Are ya satisfied? No… you gotta put more pressure on me." Then Vic raised his voice to a high pitch to mimic me, 'Vi..ic, you gotta get away from these guys, I don't like them.' So what do I do? I gotta make a truckload of money to start my own business, and real fast too, so Precious Penelope don't get herself all panicky. I had to step on a few toes to do it, and guess what baby?! I got some people really pissed off!! All I ask you to do is love me. Everything I do, I do for you. Why can't you just be happy and love me? You're ripping the heart right out of my chest and I can't take it no more! That's right baby, I'm the one that can't take it no more!"

Vic picked up a baseball bat and handed it to me, then he got down on his knees. "Baby, please, hit me, beat me with the bat, take out all of your aggressions, it'll make you feel better and you won't be mad at me no more. I can handle that kind of pain, just hit me, give me something that I can understand, something that I can deal with! Just don't break my heart no more, please baby, please!"

There are two sides to every story; in Vic's position, he was doing the best that he could. And I learned something that day, never pressure a man like this, you will push him back into crime!

Following the explosion, things changed, but not for the better. Vic drove a different car every week or so. They were never flashy cars, always older inconspicuous models.

Devastated at the loss of Inky, Vic had no measuring stick, no emotional balance or support. He was angry and out for revenge and recklessly plummeted downward, deeper and deeper into the dark life of the underworld. There was nothing that I could do to stop him. Vic wouldn't listen to me; he thought that I was naïve and quickly dismissed me and my opinion.

Even though Vic thought that he had hidden everything from me, I managed to pick up pieces of telling information. I found that I had been right about Edwin; he was an illegal drug manufacturer, and now it all belonged to Vic, and sadly he made the mistake of using his own product.

The drugs had an incomprehensible effect on Vic; they completely changed him. There wasn't much about him that was even recognizable, no sign of the kind Dr. Jekyll, he had completely disappeared, dominated by the evil and murderous Mr. Hyde.

I had managed to hold myself together through my confrontation with Edwin, but with the car bomb, and Inky's death on top of it, it was more than my fragile constitution could handle. Every day I wondered if it would be my last. Would today be the day that someone would come bursting into the house, guns blazing, and kill the both of us? I fell back into crisis, trapped in the bedroom for months, chained by the strong bonds of agoraphobia, and that was the way that Vic liked it. He professed to support my recovery, but I soon realized that it wasn't at all true. The few times that I had managed to make it out of the house, he started an argument with me and went on a rampage, throwing things and screaming, frightening me until I ran back to the bedroom, unable to breath, my heart racing, completely debilitated with another terrifying attack. Vic was like a madman; he told me that if I ever left him, he would kill me, and I believed him.

If I was ever going to get well, it would have to be without Vic's knowledge, and I learned to hide my progress from him. "One step at a time, deal with the rest later," that was my plan and I slowly regained my equanimity and strength.

It wasn't long before, Vic, had expanded his criminal organization, and I would sometimes hear him on the phone with "clients."

"Do you want his arms or legs broke? …. Oh, this guy must have really pissed you off, his arms and his legs, heh, heh, heh."

And another time, "How much does he owe you? …. I take half; it'll cost you thirty grand…. Fine, I'll send, Bruno and Big Leo…. Where can they catch this guy? … After they collect, do you want him whacked?"

I found that a human life was worth only five hundred dollars, and that these decisions were sometimes made flippantly or in anger.

I wondered how, Vic, could talk so freely on the phone about such serious crimes. Why wasn't he being more careful? He wasn't concerned at all about getting caught and I knew that there had to be a good reason for it; Vic wasn't that stupid. And one night about midnight, two FBI agents came to the house and I found out why.

Desperate for information, I stood on the stairs and listened as it was all laid out for me; Vic was working for the FBI! No wonder he was so sure of himself. No, he wasn't a rat, he was hired to carry out special assignments that the FBI couldn't dirty their hands with. If Vic got caught, no one would believe that it was sanctioned by the feds and they stood free and clear of it.

That night, Vic was hired to get information out of a terrorist. He was given the man's location, in Washington DC, and told to do whatever it took. With a wink, the agents said, "We wouldn't mind if he never turned up again."

The next morning, Vic was packing for the trip, "I've got business in DC," he told me. "I'll see ya in a couple of days." He pulled me close and kissed me good-bye. "You call Wendy if you need anything, and don't let anyone else in the house!"

Every time that Vic left, there was a part of me that wished he would never come back. But I did love the man, he cared for me and I felt bad for what he had become. Maybe it was my fault, maybe I had pushed him too hard. Or were the drugs solely responsible? Vic was never like this before drugs came into his life. But regardless of how we had gotten here, I couldn't stay with a man like this any longer, an out-of-control drug addict, a man who was a paid assassin!

Even though Vic had told me that he would kill me if I left him, I decided to take the chance! I had to get away, no matter what the cost! When he left for the airport, it was time for me to jump into action and I had to move fast. Vic said that he would be gone for a few days, but that didn't mean that it was necessarily true; he was unpredictable and I didn't know how much time I really had.

I got into the car and drove to the nearest pay phone, I called Ray, and I asked him for my job back. The first thing, Ray, did was inquire about my health. I explained about the carbon monoxide poisoning and that that had been what was causing the panic attacks. I assured him that I had recovered and was capable of holding down the job. I was happy when, Ray, wanted me back at work.

Ray knew that I had been living in Las Vegas. "Why don't you start the beginning of next month," he suggested, "that'll give you time to make the move."

"Ray, I'm in a bad relationship with a violent man, and I need to get out of town, right away." Is there anything that you can do for me?"

Ray asked me to hold the line and then came back to the phone a few minutes later. "I talked to Jan about it, and she wants you to stay here with us in the guestroom until you can get your own place. You'll be safe here."

Going back to work for Ray was one thing, staying at his house was something entirely different. I couldn't take a risk like that with Ray's home and family. "Ray, I appreciate it but my fiancé is dangerous and I don't want to be responsible if something should happen."

"Being in the business that I'm in, security is my top priority," Ray explained, "my identity and location are well buried, and no one can find me. I live in the country, the place is like a fortress and I have rifles and shotguns at every door, not to mention my six guard dogs."

"Sounds like you're ready for anything," I commented.

Ray went on, "It's a three story house, Jan and I live on the top floor where we can see clearly in all directions. Believe me, I'm not worried about this guy; you can relax, Penelope, this isn't my first rodeo, you know."

"If you're that sure Ray, I'll catch the next flight out of town. Is there a shuttle that comes out that way?"

"No, I'll send the new kid to pick you up. Call me when you know your time of arrival."

I hung up the phone, and stood there for a minute to get my bearings. I was shocked that things had gone so well. I couldn't believe that Ray had not only rehired me, but he and his wife, Jan, were actually inviting me into their home. Ray had always been adamant that his operatives be of stellar reputation; if he even suspected that they might bring personal problems to the workplace, they were quickly dealt with. The whole time that I had worked for him I made it a point not to let him know about my personal life. But things were obviously different now, the bottom line was money ... money talks and I had made a lot of it for Ray. If he was willing to take a chance with me, I would take him up on it.

I rushed home, called the airport shuttle, and packed a suitcase. It was difficult, trying to decide what to leave behind and what to take with me. The bedroom was a mess, clothes thrown all over.

I was in a hurry, fearing that I would be caught. I quickly dragged the suitcase down the stairs, thump, thump, thump, thump, and suddenly, I heard someone knocking at the door, not ringing from the gate. "It must be that blasted Wendy?!"

I shoved my suitcase into the hall closet and then opened the front door. "Hi Penelope," Wendy greeted me.

"Wendy, I'm not feeling well today, why don't you come back later?" I said trying to get rid of her.

"Sorry to hear that," Wendy said sympathetically as she pushed her way into the house. "Vic asked me to come by and see if you need anything."

Wendy wandered into the family room, looking around. "You know what an asshole he is, so suspicious. I actually have to call him tonight with my report. Can you believe it? "

Wendy had always tried to be a friend to me, as good of a friend as she could be, under the circumstances. I liked her, but when it came down to it, it was very clear that her loyalties laid with Vic.

I hoped that she would just take a quick look downstairs and then leave. If she went upstairs and saw the room in such a mess, she would immediately realize that something was wrong. Then, Vic would know about it and have someone here to stop me before I could get out of the driveway. If Wendy headed up the stairs, I would have to stop her, and that wouldn't be easy. She was a big tough, strong girl, a girl who knew the streets. She was more than I could handle, and I knew that I would have to sucker-punch her. It didn't sit well with me, I liked the woman, but the shuttle was due any minute and I didn't have time to mess around with her. I had to act fast or I wouldn't make it out.

Just as I had feared, Wendy headed up the stairs, "I'm sorry Penelope, but, Vic specifically told me to check upstairs." Vic was Wendy's employer, I couldn't blame her for what she was doing, she was just following orders, but that didn't matter, I still had to knock her out. I cringed and was just about to take the swing when suddenly, I had another idea. "Wait here Wendy," I told her, just as she reached the top landing, "I have a surprise for you." Wendy stopped and I ran into the bedroom closet and grabbed a leather coat with fur collar and cuffs. I hadn't had it altered yet, it was too big for me, so I figured that it would fit her. As I walked with the coat past the window, I looked outside and saw the airport shuttle! It had just passed the house and was headed down the road, it would be only minutes before the driver would realize his mistake, circle around and be back!

"Wendy, I bought this especially for you. Isn't it beautiful? It's Italian leather and fox fur. Why don't you try it on?" I suggested as I shuffled her back down the stairs.

"Ohhh, thank you Penelope," Wendy said breathlessly, "no one has ever given me such an expensive gift, I love it!"

"It looks great on you! I'll call ya later, maybe we can get together tomorrow, when I feel better."

"Okay," Wendy agreed, admiring the lovely coat. "Thanks again," she said as she got into her car and drove away.

I watched Wendy drive down the long driveway, "I hope she'll be okay when Vic finds out that I'm gone," I worried.

The shuttle was slowly coming back up the road, toward the house. My heart was pounding and I was shaking. "Go faster, Wendy, get the hell out of here!"

Just as Wendy went around the bend, the shuttle pulled up the driveway! I carefully placed my engagement ring on the table, ran for my suitcase and was outside waiting at the gate when the shuttle pulled up. "Get me the hell out of here... fast!" I demanded as I slipped the driver a fifty.

We were going down the long road toward the highway, and I couldn't breathe. "Hold it together, you're almost there," I told myself. The fear and tension were overwhelming me. I took little tiny breaths and wondered if I was going to have a heart attack, but when we pulled out onto the open road, suddenly I felt great. I had made it!

I got to the airport and boarded the flight, the plane took off and as it reached altitude, I felt even better.

"Vic will be upset for a while," I reasoned, "but he'll get over it. He won't be able to find me, Ray, will make sure of it, and then he'll just replace me with someone else. Maybe he'll find someone that he likes even better than me. Vic doesn't have any trouble with the ladies and there are plenty of women who want to be in my place, shouldn't be a problem for him."

When I got off of the plane, Ray's employee, was there to pick me up. His name was, Kevin, he was a nice kid and very accommodating. "I've heard all about you Miss Penelope," Kevin excitedly told me. "I couldn't believe it when, Ray, told me that I was picking you up today. Why, you're practically a living legend! The guys still talk about some of the cases that you worked, especially the Rakker case. I never thought that I would actually get the chance to ask you this in person; but is it true, what you did to those guys?"

"It's true alright kid, you can believe it. I was alone with those perverts and there was no one there to stop me. I must admit that I was out of control, if Joe hadn't come in when he did, I would have tortured them both to death."

"Man, you're a badass!" Kevin exclaimed. "Could you give me a few pointers sometime?"

"Sure kid," I said flippantly, but I must admit that it felt incredibly good to find out that someone still remembered who I was.

There was no set time for me to be at Ray's place and I asked Kevin to drive me through my old home town, just to look around. We rode down the main street, not much had changed, but I noticed a new attorney's office. "Pull in here," I told Kevin, I had decided to sue, John Stevenson, the landlord who had poisoned me.

I went into the office and the attorney, Daniel Krieger, saw me within minutes; he was just starting out and was happy to have the business.

Daniel and I reached an agreement, we both signed a contract and within the hour, I was back in the car with Kevin on my way to Ray's.

I reached, Ray and Jan's, place after dinner, we said our hellos and visited for a while. "You came back at a good time," Ray excitedly told me. "I was just saying, last week, that I could really use my secret weapon about now; I've missed ya kid. I have a case in the works that's right up your alley, undercover work. It'll be risky, but that's the way you like 'em... dangerous!"

"Ray," Jan interrupted, "can't you see that Penelope's tired? You can talk to her about it when she starts work ... the day after tomorrow! Give the girl time to catch her breath."

"Jan's right, it has been a long day," I agreed, then I excused myself and went to bed.

As I lay there, I could only hope that my wishful thinking wasn't just that, and that Vic would let me go. And that wasn't the only thing bothering me; I knew that I had been lying when I told Ray that I was capable of holding down the job. But true or not, I had to be capable, no matter how I felt. I was going to be working a dangerous case, right out the gate, and I needed all my wits about me.

Would I be able to start over again, have my job back and reclaim my life? It was a tall order; my head was spinning and I was plenty worried; I couldn't sleep all night.

The next morning, Jan was knocking at the bedroom door, "Penelope, phone call for you."

"What? A phone call for me? No one knew where I was! This couldn't be good," I said to myself as I jumped to my feet. "I'm coming Jan."

I rushed into the kitchen, "They forwarded the call from the office," Jan told me.

"Thank you Jan."

I picked up the phone, my hands were shaking, "Hello."

It was, Al, from the jewelry store, where I used to work, "Penelope, you've got to call Vic. He was here at the store, waiting for me when I opened up this morning. He left me the phone number at the hotel where he's staying. He told me that he's going to get crazier and crazier until he has you back, and that people are going to start getting hurt! My answering machine is full of messages from your friends and relatives looking for you, he's called and threatened them all! I can't believe how terrible he looks, almost like he's out of his mind!"

"Al, he is out of his mind, he's on drugs and dangerous; don't take any chances with him. If he shows up again, shoot him! Al knew how to handle himself, but I thought that I had better let him know what he was dealing with.

Well, the jig was up, Vic, wasn't going to let me go, all of my hopes were dashed. I couldn't believe how quickly he had tracked me down. He had even gone to the right person, Al. Al never threw away anything; he had Ray's phone number from my old job application and had found me within minutes.

I jotted down the phone and room number of Vic's hotel and after apologizing to Al, I hung up. I couldn't let Vic hurt someone and it was only a matter of time before he would.

"Jan, my fiancé is already in town making trouble, I have to go see him, right away!"

"Penelope, listen, let's talk to Ray first, maybe he can do something."

"No Jan, as much as I appreciate it I can't get Ray involved; he doesn't know who he's dealing with. I'm going to call Kevin, and see if he can drive me."

I called Kevin, and explained the situation. He rushed out to Ray's and picked me up. I had him drop me near the hotel where Vic was staying, but out of sight of it. I gave the kid a few bucks and thanked him before I sent him on his way. As Kevin drove off, I wondered if Vic would make good his promise to kill me, and if Kevin would be the last person to see me alive.

I thought about calling Vic, and meeting him in a public place, but then decided to walk over to the hotel. Whatever I had to do would have to be done in private, not with a dozen witnesses. "Maybe if I catch him by surprise, it'll be to my advantage." I was forcing my legs to walk and it was as though they were fighting me every step of the way. I didn't know what would happen when I got to Vic's room, but whatever it was, I was going to deal with it. If I didn't stop him now, I knew that he would do just what he had promised, he would get crazier and crazier and people would get hurt. That was the only thing that I could be sure of.

I went up the elevator and walked down the hall, pulling my suitcase along. People greeted me as we passed, I smiled and said hello, but I felt like I was in another world. I reached the room, number 204, this was it; I took a breath and knocked on the door. I heard some rustling, and then the door opened and Vic grabbed me, pulled me just inside and pressed me against the wall. He kissed me and clutched me tightly while he kicked the door shut, and then pushed me to the bed. "Maybe Vic loved me enough, maybe he wouldn't make good his threat to kill me and it would be alright."

Vic was on top of me kissing me, but then he stopped and slowly stood up, looking down at me lying on the bed. I knew that this was it… Vic pulled a knife from his pocket, and I pulled out the Beretta, that I had taken from Edwin. I knew better than to pull a weapon and not use it immediately, but I couldn't bring myself to pull the trigger and I held it on him.

"Hey Baby, you're overreacting, I was just taking it out of my pants," he held the knife up, "see, it ain't even open." Vic threw the knife on the bed and then he unbuckled his belt and unzipped his pants. I continued to hold the gun on him as I watched him undress. As Vic took off his clothes, my mind thought of nothing, nothing but wanting him. "Heaven help me, what kind of a freak am I?! Shoot him you idiot!!!"

Vic acted as though the gun wasn't there, he climbed on the bed and kissed my neck, his soft whiskers tickled and sent a shiver down my spine, then he reached for my blouse and began to unbutton it. "Maybe it wouldn't hurt to have sex with him, just one more time, for old time's sake," I reasoned. I slowly lowered the gun to my side, "I'll shoot him later."

Once again, Vic and I made love like we always did, and it was like it always was … incredible, the man was phenomenal. What was it about him? No matter what horrible things he did or what happened between us, the sex was always fantastic, beyond belief. I couldn't understand it. I always wanted him, he was my addiction, like a shot of heroin coursing through my veins; he took me to paradise every single time.

When it was over and I had caught my breath, I decided to try reasoning with him. "Vic, I apologize for leaving the way I did; it was wrong, but I tried to talk to you and you wouldn't listen to me. I can't go on like this; I want to stay here and start my life over. Please just go home without me; we can still get together once in a while."

When Vic heard what I had said to him, he slipped his heavy hand around my throat, he didn't hurt me, but he looked me in the eyes, "Baby, you ain't going nowhere." His voice was so low that it didn't sound human, it was as though a demonic force was threatening me. I had never seen this side of him before and it scared me to the bone. "You belong to me, and you'll be with me until I say different!" He then released me and opened the night table drawer; he pulled out my engagement ring and put it back on my finger. "Now get dressed, we're going back to Vegas." And we did.

When we reached Las Vegas, Tank, one of Vic's crew, was waiting for us at the house. Tank took my suitcase from the trunk of Vic's car and asked, "Do you want me to stay here and keep an eye on her?"

"No, you're coming with me, she ain't going to go nowhere today, she's too tired, come on inside."

We all went in the house and Vic and Tank walked into the family room and lined up their dope. I took a bottle of water from the refrigerator and went upstairs to bed. Vic was right, I was too tired to go anywhere. I climbed under the covers and lay there, looking up at the ceiling. I had failed, I was right back where I started, but at least I had been able to feel like my old self again… if only for a little while.

Vic was doing drugs, when he should have been sleeping, he had already been up for three days, and he would be even crazier by the time he got home that night.

I fearfully remembered a horrific thing that happened to my friend, Brad, in high school. Brad had been doing drugs like Vic, and hadn't slept for four days when he started to hallucinate. He thought that his father was a vampire that was trying to kill him. Brad ran into the garage and hid there, holding an axe in his hands. When his unaware father entered, Brad attacked and brutally chopped his father into pieces.

I went to visit, Brad, in the mental hospital. Once the drugs wore off and he had had some sleep, he came out of it. But Brad couldn't live with what he had done to his adoring father and he was never the same.

These drugs were dangerous and I knew it; Vic was cranked up with no sleep and I was deathly afraid of him. I wished that I had shot him at the hotel, but I just couldn't bring myself to do it; I couldn't shoot Vic any more than I could shoot myself. Yes, it was a sorry situation, but true, I loved the man and I couldn't bring myself to hurt him.

After I heard Tank and Vic leave the house, I fell asleep. A few hours later, I was awakened by someone knocking at the front door. I couldn't believe it! "Can't anyone ever leave me alone! It's probably that stupid Wendy wanting a piece of me. I've had all I can stand!"

I stomped down stairs and opened the door, expecting a confrontation with Wendy, but it was the cable guy. "I'm here to hook up the cable," he said.

"I don't want cable, get lost!" I sneered and went back upstairs to the bedroom. Now I was awake, I sat on the edge of the bed and held my head in my hands. "What am I going to do? It's hopeless," I sobbed.

Suddenly, I heard a voice, "Oh, come on Penelope, let me hook you up."

I slowly looked up from my despair at a man leaning in the doorway of my bedroom. First I saw his boots, then my eyes climbed, his hips were cocked and his thumbs were hooked in his tool belt. He had a nice pair of shoulders on him and a well-developed chest. Then I saw his face, his magnificent blue eyes and dark shiny hair falling on his forehead. "Wait a minute, I recognize this guy. But who is he?"

I didn't have to wonder for long, when the mystery man started swinging his hips and singing to me. He was the Elvis impersonator from the casino!

"What in the world are you doing here Elvis?" I asked. I didn't get an answer right away, Elvis was such a ham that he had to finish the entire song before he would speak to me. I sat and watched him shimmying and shaking and singing me a love song. He was a real mood lifter.

When he had finished his performance, I got up, "Come on, let's go downstairs."

We went to the kitchen and I opened the refrigerator and asked if he wanted something to drink.

"Hey Mama, when you offered a drink, I thought you meant a real drink," he said and flipped his hair back.

"Okay, let's have a real drink."

I took a bottle of tequila from the cupboard and cut a lime. "Grab the salt," I instructed as I poured us each a shot. We both walked into the living room, where I could see the driveway. From that position, I knew that I would have enough time to cover things up before Vic could get up the driveway and through the gate.

Elvis and I drank down the first shot; I had the bottle in my hand and poured us another. "Now, why don't you tell me what in the world you're doing here, posing as a cable guy?"

"I had a few days before I start a new gig in Florida," he explained.

"So you just decided to become a cable guy for a few days?"

"No, no now honey, I used to work for the cable company, the owner's a friend of mine. He needed a hand and I decided to help him out before I left town."

"That's nice," I replied as I poured us yet another shot, and that was the beginning. Elvis and I drank and laughed all afternoon. I was having a great time, but always on my mind was the dreaded the moment when Vic would come home.

Elvis asked me to dance, he was singing and shimmying up and down, running his hands along the curves of my body. We were both a little tipsy by this time and I stumbled toward him. He caught me, but then we both lost our balance and fell on the sofa. Elvis was on top of me and things suddenly became intense; he reached for my chin and turned my head toward him to try and kiss me, but I pushed him away and then sat up. Elvis put his arm around me, "Now don't you think that it's about time that you told me what's wrong."

"Come on now Elvis, let's not let my problems ruin our fun," I said, trying to keep things light, but it didn't work.

Elvis went on, "Penelope, I remember the very first time that I saw you. You and Vic had just pulled into town and you came to see my show. You were absolutely stunning, so happy and full of life, but I knew that it was just a matter of time before you would be dragged down. You can't be around these people for long before the dirt starts rubbing off on you. I've been working at the casino for a few years now, and I learned it the hard way. That's why I'm leaving. The money's great and I have a good following…"

"Yeah, you sure do have a lot of fans," I interrupted, "I noticed the women mobbing you after your show." I was trying to change the subject, I just wanted to have a good time with this guy, not hear all of this dramatic crap.

"You really did notice?" Elvis asked surprised, "Why didn't you ever talk to me?"

"I wasn't going to stand up there with the rest of the screwballs and make a fool of myself."

"Oh really, so my fans are screwballs?" Elvis said playfully.

"If you wanted to talk, why didn't you just talk to me?" I asked.

"You don't know?"

"Don't know what?"

"No one's allowed to talk to you, unless you speak to them first. The boss sent out the order, he didn't want anyone hitting on you."

"That figures," I said irritated, "those guys are overprotective. Well now's your chance, is there something that you've been wanting to say?"

"Only that I've been standing by; I couldn't even approach you. I was hoping that someday you would speak to me, but it never happened. I was upset when I sang to you at the engagement party. I knew that you were making a dreadful mistake, but I couldn't say or do anything to stop you. Penelope, you don't belong with these people!"

"I remember that night," I said grinning, "you almost fell off the stage. I knew that something was up, but I never dreamed that it had anything to do with me."

"Well it did, it had everything to do with you. I've been admiring you from afar, watching you plummet to your ruin with no way to help, and now fate has brought us together. I always wondered what you were like, and now I know; precious and sweet, just like I imagined. Penelope, would you come to Florida with me?"

"Maybe I didn't hear you right. Did you just ask me to go to Florida?"

"Yes you heard me right," he confirmed. "I know all about Vic and his crew, I know what they are and I'm not afraid of them. Let me take you out of here, right now, we can have a great life together."

Elvis knew what he was getting into when he asked me to go with him. Even if he was drunk and came to his senses the next day, it was still a way out. Tomorrow, Tank, would be watching me and it would be too late. "My bag is already packed, let's go!"

The next thing I knew, Elvis and I were in his convertible racing down the highway!

"What's your real name anyway," I asked as the wind whipped through my hair, "I can't keep calling you Elvis."

"You're gonna have to unless you think of a name you like better, my name really is Elvis."

"Well, that makes it easy," I replied.

We had driven for several hours when Elvis told me that he had to stop and see his mother. "We can spend the night at her place and leave in the morning; it's getting late."

"That's nice of you to offer, but I'd really rather not. You go ahead and spend time with your mother, I don't want to interfere. Not a good idea for her to know about me anyway; I'll stay at a hotel."

"I'm not leaving you alone all night, I'll go and see my mother in the morning and you can sleep in."

"Sounds like a plan."

Elvis pulled the car over to a hotel, just off the exit, "This okay? There's not much choice in this little town."

"This will be fine, it looks like a nice place."

Elvis and I entered the hotel and walked up to the desk. He gave the clerk his credit card, but the hotel didn't accept that particular card. "I like to use it because of the low interest," Elvis explained, "but that's fine I'll just use another card."

As Elvis thumbed through his unorganized wallet, I quickly pulled out my credit card and handed it to the clerk, "Here, just put it on this one."

"No way," Elvis protested, "I'm paying for this!"

"No, I'm the one that wanted to stay at a hotel, so I'm paying for it."

As Elvis and I argued, the clerk ran the card, "We're not going to make this man go through the trouble of crediting my account, just forget about it," I said, as I signed the charge slip. "It's no big deal."

"Well okay, but everything else is on me," Elvis proclaimed as he hugged my shoulders.

I didn't even know this guy and somehow I believed that he was sincere. But, I could always be wrong. Maybe it was just the thrill of tasting forbidden fruit, or stealing a woman from a notorious mobster. Was Elvis an adrenalin junky? At this point, it really didn't matter to me, I was on my way to Florida. I had no ties to Florida and Vic would never find me there!

Elvis and I relaxed on the bed and ordered room service then, we watched a movie and kissed and cuddled. As things heated up, I was getting uncomfortable; I had never had sex with a stranger before. But this was different, this man had a lot of courage and he was taking an incredible risk for me. We were together now, and even though I didn't even know him, Elvis was my new man. Yes, he was sexy, there was no doubt about that, but I still didn't expect another man to measure up to

Vic, and I was prepared to be disappointed. I decided not to postpone the inevitable and force myself to get it over with, "Come here, big boy," I said as I pulled him toward me. I prepared to fake the whole thing, "Just be happy that he's the young, good-looking Elvis, and not the old fat one," I whispered to myself.

Elvis didn't need any more coaxing, that man was on me and he was a wild one! Much to my surprise, I was actually enjoying myself; he was great! Not surprising, he had a lot of rhythm and there was something about that consistent rhythmic Elvis motion that got to me, and I didn't have to fake anything!

"You know what Elvis, I think we're going to be just fine," I happily declared.

"You're right, I finally have my dream girl," he said, in reply as we sweetly fell asleep in each other's arms.

The next morning, Elvis quietly tiptoed around the room, trying not to wake me. He was meticulous with his grooming and it took him over an hour and a half to get ready. When he was finally dressed, he knocked over his aftershave and the bottle crashed loudly on the counter. "Sorry I woke ya darlin," he apologized. "I'm gonna go visit my mother now," he said, and then sweetly kissed me good-bye. "I'll be back in a few hours, get some rest and we'll leave after lunch."

"Sounds good," I responded.

I smiled as I fell back to sleep, I was happy, I had a good life to look forward to. "I'll probably have a lot of fun with Elvis."

Moments later, I was awakened by a knock at the door, "It must be Elvis! He probably forgot something." I happily leapt from the bed and opened the door, "Good morning El…" But it wasn't Elvis, it was Wendy standing there! I was terrified!

She pushed her way into the room and started throwing my belongings into my suitcase. "Come on Penelope, we have the move fast, Vic is ready to blow!"

"How in the world did you find me?"

"You used your credit card, and the time before that, you bought an airline ticket. The damn feds don't mind doing favors for Vic; they'll track you down for him every time. There's no way that you're ever going to get away, so do me a favor and make both of our lives easier, please, just stay home! Vic tore the house apart, the whole downstairs is in shambles; he busted furniture and smashed dishes, and punched holes in the walls."

Suddenly, Wendy stopped, smelling the men's cologne, then she noticed Elvis' clothes. "Are you crazy, having a man in here? We've got to do something about this guy; we don't want Vic to find out about him! You know what will happen if he handles it!"

"You're right, Wendy, I'll leave him a note."

"Dear Elvis, I've changed my mind and decided to go back to Vic, I still love him. Please don't ever contact me." It was a cruel note, but I didn't want Elvis to come looking for me. Like Wendy said, I knew what would happen if Vic handled it.

I got dressed, and Wendy had my things packed in minutes. "When we get to the car," she instructed, "whatever you do, don't say a word to Vic. He's in the back seat and I'm driving, just get in the front with me."

Wendy and I left the room together. "I'm sorry that I to put you through this Wendy, hope you didn't get in too much trouble the last time I left.

"Don't worry about it, the coat made up for it."

"So we're cool?"

"Yeah, we're cool," Wendy assured me, "I could never stay mad at you."

Vic didn't speak to me the whole way home; the trip was tense and uncomfortable. I knew that I had pushed him too far and I was afraid of what he was going to do to me when we got home. But, when we did get home, he didn't do anything; he simply walked inside and went straight upstairs, still without speaking a word.

Wendy carried my suitcase and came inside with me; the house was a disaster, just as she had described. "I'm going to start cleaning up down here," she told me.

"I'll help you," I offered.

"No way, Vic's not going to let, his baby, clean up this shit. You better get upstairs with him."

With that, I climbed the stairs and entered the bedroom to see Vic already lying in bed. I took a bath and then climbed in beside him. Vic rolled over and put his arms around me, he pulled me close and finally spoke, "Now I can get some sleep," and within seconds he was fast asleep.

I laid there listening to Wendy downstairs; she had called a crew to help her and they worked all night long, cleaning and repairing. As the hours passed, I fearfully laid in Vic's arms thinking about my situation. The way I saw it, I had two choices, I had to kill Vic or stay with him. Those were my only options because he would never let me go. I had already tried to shoot him once and couldn't bring myself to do it, so I resigned myself to staying with him and hoped that I would survive.

When the sun rose the next morning, somehow I felt more calm, and I was finally able to get to sleep. Vic slept right along with me, and we didn't wake up until noon. When Vic opened his eyes, I was fearful again, wondering what he would do, but he surprised me and acted like there was nothing wrong. I could feel an angry undercurrent, but figured that as long as I didn't push his buttons, it might be okay. So, I played along.

Vic always counted on sex to solve all of our problems and today was no exception; he asked me to join him in the shower. I stepped into the large marble shower and Vic rubbed slick bubbly soap all over my body, then we made hot steamy love. It was a great stress relief and I did feel better afterward; at least I knew that he still desired me.

After we dressed, we went downstairs and a delivery van was pulling away, Wendy had bought new furniture. "I couldn't get the same sofa, I hope that this one is okay," she explained.

Before Vic could speak, I answered, "Of course it is Wendy, it's perfect."

"That's not my department, whatever you girls say," Vic said shaking his head as he walked to the kitchen.

I discreetly slipped a hundred dollar bill into Wendy's hand, "Thanks for covering for me Wendy," I whispered and she nodded in reply.

While Vic was drinking his coffee, he sent Wendy home. A few minutes later, Tank and Big Leo, showed up and waited for him on the front porch. Vic kissed me good-bye, "Tank's your bodyguard now," he told me; then Vic and Big Leo got in the car and drove away, leaving Tank behind on the porch.

Now it was official, I was a prisoner and that's how it went; when Vic wasn't home, Tank was sitting on the porch. Wendy ran all of my errands and I never went anywhere unless it was with Vic. Strangely enough, it didn't bother me much. I buried myself in my artwork and when there wasn't any more room in the house to hang paintings, I started designing greeting cards. They were small and didn't take up much room and I enjoyed drawing the pictures and writing the verse.

Vic and I went out regularly. I think that he was trying to recapture the excitement of our early relationship, but it never worked. He was on drugs and something would always happen to make him angry. If a man looked at my legs or the waiter took too long to take our order, it would send him into a rage and someone always called the police. I can't count the number of times that we left a nightclub or restaurant, hearing the sirens of police cars on the way. It was insane.

Things were never the same between Vic and me, I had left him and he was holding a grudge. He got angry with me at the slightest little thing, turning into a madman, punching holes in the walls, breaking furniture and smashing dishes. Wendy and her crew always cleaned it up and our fights soon became notorious, everyone knew about them. It had become a joke, "If you two could just learn to fuck and fight at the same time, you'd have it made."

And that was just the beginning, Vic got worse and worse, doing more and more drugs. The longer it went on, the more insane and paranoid he became. Vic didn't look the same, he lost weight and had dark circles under his eyes and his face even began to have a hollow look.

It was terrifying living with Vic; he had never laid a hand on me, but I knew that it was just a matter of time before he would. He was like a powerful seething volcano building up pressure and I knew that when he finally did blow, it would be the end. The fact that he loved me, was little consolation, I lived in a state of constant fear and tension, remembering every day what my friend, Brad, had done to his father, someone that he had dearly loved.

I didn't know how much more of it I could take. There were nights when I prayed that the police would come and arrest us. Prison had to be better than the way that I was living! Sadly, that was the best I could hope for … prison.

One night, Vic and I went to see a show at the casino. A famous classical pianist was performing there, and I was looking forward to enjoying the soothing lovely music. The night started off pleasantly, as it usually did, but when I got out of the car, the valet bumped me with the door and it snagged my stocking. I didn't say anything to Vic; I didn't know if he would go nuts over it, I could never predict what would set him off.

Once we were seated, I tried to find the snag to determine how bad it looked. I ran my hand up my leg examining it and didn't see anything, but the man sitting next to me noticed. He thoughtlessly touched my leg with his finger, "There it is," he told me, pointing out the snag and smiling.

That was it, Vic went into a rage, the man stood up and Vic reached over me and punched him in the face, knocking him over several rows of seats. Blood splattered on people and everyone began to scream and scramble away. Vic grabbed the man again and dragged him to the front of the concert hall. The ushers were on their way, running down the aisle shouting and ordering Vic to stop.

"Afraid your show is going to get ruined?" Vic angrily shouted back at them. "Let me help you out, here's a stand-in for ya!" Vic picked up the unconscious man and threw him on the stage. His bloody body landed on the bench and the grand piano thundered as he fell slumped over on the keys. The sound resonated through the concert hall and I could feel the vibration. The eerie image of the bloody limp man at the piano, gripped the remaining people in the theatre and they all stood motionless.

By this time, the boys were there and they all jumped on Vic. Once they had a hold of him, Vic started trying to pull himself together and explain why he had done it. "You guys understand, he touched my ol' lady! Any one of you would have done the same thing!"

I didn't know what the boys had planned; maybe this was it for Vic! There was nothing that I could do about it, so I just quietly followed behind as they dragged, Vic, away. The boys took, Vic, to the back of the casino. I wondered if they would shoot him there, but they didn't, they just threw him out into the street. "The boss don't want no druggies around here. Show up again, and you get a bullet in the head."

I had started to walk out the door after Vic, when Ross, one of the boys, stopped me. I didn't know Ross very well, but he was concerned, "What are you doing? You can't leave with this crazy, he's liable to kill ya, just stay here!"

"I can't stay here, if I do, he'll come back and you'll have to shoot him."

There wasn't much time to talk, so Ross got right to it, "If you ever want to leave Vic, I've got a place where you can hide out."

I was completely beside myself with Vic, living with the tension and fighting, a hideout sounded pretty good to me. "What do you mean; you have somewhere to hide out?

"I have a place in Laguna and I'm hardly ever there."

"What's in it for you?" I asked.

"I need someone to housesit; I don't like leaving the place empty. You'd be doing me a favor," Ross explained.

"Sounds good Ross, but I'm not getting into some sex slave thing with you, just housesitting…. Right?"

"No strings attached," Ross promised.

I wasn't sure if I could take him at his word, but considering the alternative, I decided to go for it. "Okay Ross, here's the plan, there's a big boulder, about fifty yards down the road past Vic's, park behind it and wait for me there, you can't be seen from the house. Noon will be a good time, Vic, will have left for work long before then and I'll be ready."

"I'll be there," Ross assured me and with that, I shook his hand and left.

Vic was waiting for me in the car, I climbed in and we and drove away. All I had to do was make it through one more night, and then the next morning, somehow make my escape from Tank.

The night was exceptionally tense; I hoped that it wouldn't be the night that, Vic, would go into a drug-crazed frenzy and kill me. Being rejected by the boss was a big deal and I didn't know how he would handle it.

I was lucky, Vic, had other things on his mind besides me. When we got home, he called a meeting and began to restructure his organization. That made it easier for me, and I started to prepare for my escape. I packed a small backpack with toiletries and a few clothes and decided to take my greeting cards along, hoping that I could do something with them. When I finished packing, I slipped the backpack under the bed. I didn't expect Vic to look there, but I was still worried that something unusual might happen and he would. I was relieved, when later that night, he climbed into bed and went straight to sleep.

As Vic lay sleeping, I tried to devise my escape plan. I thought about going into the basement and pretending that I was hurt. I could call for Tank and when he came down to help me; I would hit him with something and then lock him down there. But I rejected that plan; they didn't call him Tank for nothing. What if I couldn't hit him hard enough and it just pissed him off, or what if I hit him too hard and killed the guy? It was just too risky. Then I remembered the big rope in the garage and decided to take another approach, climb down the cliff at the back of the house. I wasn't sure exactly how high the cliff actually was, but it was definitely no joke; I could easily plunge to my death. I was plenty scared, but it was the only way that I could be certain to get around Tank.

The next morning, Vic was up early and I expected that he would be gone quickly, as he always was. But then I smelled bacon frying and heard him on the phone laughing. Vic never ate breakfast at home, he rarely even drank a cup of coffee, this was definitely unusual behavior. Was Vic planning to stay home today? Today of all days? I laid in bed tense, and tension soon turned into panic, perhaps someone had told Vic about Ross and me! Was he waiting to confront Ross?

I quietly listened and when I heard Tank arrive, I was happy, Vic would soon be gone! It was on! Immediately, I dressed and anxiously waited for Vic to get in his car and pull out of the garage, but he didn't. Instead, he and Tank slowly walked around the yard having a lengthy discussion about a dead plant in the flowerbed. Since when were these guys concerned about a dead flower?! It was completely unbelievable, they had never shown any interest whatsoever in the garden before, and now they were examining every plant and talking about fertilizer!

It seemed to take forever, but Vic finally did finish his inspection of the garden and leave. The minute he cleared the driveway, I ran to the garage to get the long rope, but it was gone! I searched the garage and couldn't find it anywhere, but what I did find was a long orange extension cord. I ran out to the back yard and tied it around a palm tree, and then threw it over the edge of the cliff. I laid on my belly, scooted to the edge and looked down, after being wrapped around the palm tree and then running the distance across the ground, the cord only went a short way over. I would have to find more things to add on. I rummaged through the house and found more extension cords, little four and six foot lengths, I added them to the orange cord, but still not even close.

Tank wasn't allowed to step foot inside the house, he used the bathroom in the backyard by the pool; if he was going to catch me, that would be how. I peeked out on the front porch to check on him. Tank was intently reading a magazine, so I left the extension cords hanging from the palm tree and kept searching the house. I took the sheets from the linen closet and pulled the sheets from the bed; I tore them into wide strips and I tied them together, but after I added them on, still not long enough, the drop was way too far.

This was taking too much time! I didn't know if Ross would wait for me! I was about to give up, but then I noticed the lamp cords. Vic had bought some stained glass, swag lamps from Germany and they had long chains on them. I cut the chains off and then hurriedly pulled and cut every cord from every lamp in the house and added them on too. When I threw the cords over the edge, it was still a deadly drop to the bottom of the cliff.

It looked like I would have to abandon my plan and figure out what to tell Vic about the torn sheets and ruined lamps. The thought of facing him made me tremble, Vic went berserk over the slightest things and I had destroyed his expensive lamps! It would also be obvious to him that I was trying to leave again and I knew what I would be facing. I couldn't give up, there just had to be a way! I desperately rushed down to the basement and started digging through the boxes stored there. I opened a huge box marked Christmas, it was filled with stuffing and fragile ornaments, but I didn't care, I was in a hurry and I dumped them out, breaking them on the floor. Under the ornaments, I found strands and strands of Christmas lights! The lights were old and worn, I didn't know how strong they were, but I had to take the chance!

The lights were tangled in a massive knot and as I struggled to get them straightened, I heard Tank, he was getting up and heading for the backyard! I ran through the house and beat him there, "Tank, I'm in the spa, don't come back here!

"Okay, let me know when you're done," he replied.

Now Tank was waiting to use the bathroom and I couldn't screw around anymore! I tied the mangled Christmas lights to the last lamp cord and threw it over the edge. It was still a long way to the bottom of the cliff, but time was running out and I was desperate. "It'll stretch out when I get my weight on it," I told myself, "hopefully it'll get me close enough to jump." I figured that I would get hurt; it was still a very long drop, but the odds of me surviving the jump were better than the odds of facing Vic. I put on my backpack, grabbed hold of the orange extension cord, and backed toward the edge. I began to panic and I started to get dizzy, "Don't look down," I said to myself, "just keep going!" My boots slipped against the sandy rock cliff, but I managed to keep my footing. I kept moving downward, hand over hand and everything was going great, until I hit the Christmas lights. I grabbed the huge knot by the handful, trying to get as many strands in my hands as I could, hoping that it would hold my weight, but then the lights started to unravel and I found myself plummeting toward the ground. I remember hearing the click, click, click, click, click as each light glanced past the other. Glass was breaking, I closed my eyes and turned my head as I desperately held on. Suddenly, I jerked and came to an abrupt halt. When I looked up at the light strand, I could see that it was stretching, bare wires were exposed and it was about to break, I was going to fall! I quickly looked down to determine where I would jump and found that I was only about six feet from the ground! I let go and landed on my feet just as the jumbled mess of cords fell to the earth beside me. "Close call!" I said, and then ran to find Ross.

When I got behind the boulder, Ross wasn't there. "Okay, I took too long and Ross left me. Now what do I do?" I was already out of the house and there was no way that I was going back. I didn't know where I was headed, but I started to hike down the long road to the highway. "I'll figure it out as I go," I whispered.

I had only walked a few yards when, Ross, pulled up from behind, he stopped the car and I jumped inside.

"I had to circle around," he explained, "a cop came down the road snooping, and I got warrants out on me."

"No kidding, I just climbed down the cliff; it's a miracle that he didn't notice me either."

"Down the cliff? That's like climbing down fuckin' Mt. Everest! I guess you really meant it when you said that you wanted to get away. Today must be our lucky day, the cops didn't pick up either one of us!"

ENZO

Ross and I headed down the road, and when we pulled out onto the highway I felt relieved, just as I had the times before. I hoped that this time would be different and that I would make good my escape.

"I hope you don't mind, but we're going to drive straight through to Laguna," Ross told me. "I'm having a friend and his ol' lady over for dinner; he's got a business opportunity to discuss with me. So far, it sounds pretty good and I wanna hear what he has to say, I need something to invest in."

"That's fine with me Ross, I prefer to drive straight through."

Ross told me about his house, "You're gonna love living there, the place has an ocean view and a huge deck. The Rolls and Jag are in the garage and you can drive them any time. I've got a gardener that comes every week so, there won't be no yard work or anythin'. You'll really just be cleaning up after yourself. I'll leave ya plenty of money so you can live it up!"

"I certainly don't have any complaints so far," I happily commented, "sounds like the perfect job."

When we got to the house the guests were already there, a big handsome man named Enzo and his beautiful blonde girlfriend, Carrie. I followed Ross upstairs and he put my backpack in his bedroom. It didn't sit well with me, I had already told Ross that I didn't want to get into a sex thing with him and it looked like he was already planning to push me into it. I couldn't make an issue of it until I was sure; perhaps Ross was going to sleep in another room and let me have the master bedroom for myself. I decided to let it go until he actually tried to put the moves on me, but still, I dreaded it.

The four of us had a nice dinner, and then the men went to the living room to talk business. Carrie excused herself and went up to bed, and I decided to join the men. I listened to Enzo's proposal; his plan was to build an extravagant restaurant in Laguna. Not just any restaurant, what he had in mind was elegance, like in the old days, big band music, a shiny dance floor and a glamorous torch singer. He wanted it to be a place where the guests would dress in lovely gowns and tuxedoes and drink champagne while they dined on decadent food. Enzo planned to have the employees costumed like old-time gangsters and their molls. "You'd be perfect for that, Penelope," he said with a smile, "you've got attitude."

Enzo already had a location tied up; he had all the permits and two other investors. "We should be up and running in two months, three at the most," he told Ross. "The place already has a commercial kitchen and will only need minimal remodeling and there's a perfect set up for the dance floor and bandstand."

Ross decided that he wanted to get in on the ground floor and he told Enzo that he would have the cash for him in the morning.

Once the details of the business deal had been worked out, the conversation became more friendly. I noticed that Enzo was wearing a distinctive ring and I complimented him on it. He held up his hand to proudly display it, and told me that it was his Super Bowl ring. Enzo explained that he had been a pro football player and played the Super Bowl.

"I guess that I should have known that," I said, "but, I don't watch football. But, I used to play it when I was a kid," I added laughingly.

"Oh, so you're one of those tomboys huh," Enzo smiled. "I've always had a weakness for tomboys. There was a girl in my neighborhood growing up, kicked my ass every day and I loved the hell out of her." Enzo was a fun-loving, charming man and we hit it off.

It had been mentioned at dinner, that I was hiding at Ross' place from my crazy fiancé, and Enzo inquired as to what my plans were. I told him that I had designed some greeting cards, but hadn't done anything with them yet. "Do you have them with you?" he asked, "I'd like to take a look at them."

"Sure that would be fine," I said, and then went upstairs and retrieved my backpack. I set it on the floor and pulled out the greeting cards.

Enzo looked at each one of them and chuckled at the punch lines. "These are very good, I'd be happy to have them printed for you when I have the menus printed up for the restaurant. I'll just make it a package deal."

"Oh, that's wonderful!" I exclaimed in delight. Something was finally going right for me!

"We can even set up a display for them by the cash register," he added.

"My first customer," I giggled and shook his hand. I was delighted that someone was actually trying to help me get ahead, not hold me down.

After that, Enzo, and I began to get chummy. I told him a little bit about my work history and it wasn't long before he offered me the manager's position at his restaurant. "We'll work something out so that asshole boyfriend of yours won't be able to find you," he promised. "There's plenty of ways to hide a persons' identity."

I was thrilled! It was going to be a fantastic restaurant and Enzo promised to pay me top dollar!

We had just begun to work out the details, when Ross got up and started for the stairs. "Come on, Penelope, we're going to bed now," he boldly declared.

"I'm going to stay up and talk to Enzo," I told him, and with that, Ross angrily stormed upstairs.

"What's his problem?" Enzo questioned.

"He really does have a problem," I told Enzo, "we agreed before I came here that it wasn't going to be a sex thing; I was just going to be the house sitter, but now it looks like he's reneging on the deal."

Enzo was heated, "You're in a very vulnerable position and he's trying to take advantage of you! My God, he's treating you like a prostitute! I hate men like that, if he's that unscrupulous, I don't want anything to do with him! He can forget the whole damn business deal!"

Ross stormed back downstairs, he walked past us without saying a word and went to the garage. Enzo and I heard a car start and then screeching tires as Ross pulled out of the driveway. He stopped in front of the house, yelled something, and then screeched the tires again as he drove off.

Enzo and I looked at each other concerned; "I guess it's time to leave," he stated.

Suddenly I felt desperate, what was Ross going to do when he came back and I was alone with him?

"The guy's crazy jealous!" Enzo exclaimed as he stood up, "I can't leave you here with him, he's liable to hurt you! You're coming with me! Get ready, I'll go get Carrie."

I was relieved that Enzo was taking me with him and I waited downstairs while he went to wake Carrie. A few minutes later, he came back alone, "Carrie's staying here," he told me.

"Doesn't she know what's going on?"

"I told her, but she doesn't care. If she wants Ross, she can have him!"

Enzo and I got in his car and left. "Now where do we go?" I asked as we drove down the dark road.

"I have a friend who has a place in Mexico, Emily, you might know her. She's having a weekend party and invited Carrie and me, that's where we'll go."

I was concerned about leaving the United States, but I had heard of Emily; she was known as a standup person. Whenever the boys got out of the joint, and were on parole, she always helped them out by putting them to work at her ranch. I felt safe going to her place; Emily knew how to keep her mouth shut. "It sounds like we're off to Mexico!" I said enthusiastically.

Enzo and I drove for hours down the coast, further and further into

Mexico, it was just after sunrise when we pulled off the main road. Enzo drove past a restaurant and resort area and then turned on a narrow dirt lane. When we got to the end, I saw an incredible villa, but the place was abandoned and securely locked with bars and padlocks.

"Great, we came all this way for nothing," I whispered to myself in defeat.

The situation didn't detour Enzo; he opened the trunk of the car and took out a crowbar; he broke the bars loose and pried open the front door. "Emily must have been delayed; I'll fix the door and lock the place back up when we leave."

The heavy ornate door creaked as Enzo pushed it open. I peered in; the huge stately manor was shadowy and dark. I stepped inside and when my boots hit the floor, the sound echoed through the large rooms and hallways.

Wait here," Enzo instructed, and then found his way across the room and opened draperies that covered the tall windows. The sunlight burst into the room and the place magically lit up; sparkling crystal chandeliers, cast colorful "rainbows" around the room. The place was incredible, like a palace, towering vaulted ceilings, solid wood beams with long golden chains holding the magnificent lighting. The heavy draperies were made of velvet, and detailed tapestries portraying hunting scenes adorned the walls. The furniture was over a thousand years old, obtained from an ancient castle and the floors were made of solid slabs of the finest marble. As we walked through the magnificent villa, I looked for evidence that the place belonged to Emily; a photograph, clothing, but there was nothing, not even a bottle of perfume.

Once we had viewed the inside, Enzo showed me the back of the property. There were three huge terraces, stair stepping down to the ocean, each one bigger than the last. A mysterious mist filled the air; it was as though I was in an imaginary world.

It had been a long stressful day; Enzo and I had been up all night and the utmost thing on my mind was sleep. I walked up the wide spooky staircase to a bedroom and found a fluffy quilt. Then I went outside to a shaded area on the last terrace closest to the ocean. I wrapped up in the warm quilt and laid on a lounge chair, watching the roaring waves crash on the jagged rock cliffs. After living in the desert, the moist clean air was heavenly, I breathed in deeply, fully enjoying it for a few moments, but soon my thoughts became worried. How could I relax? Enzo had broken into this villa!

I was restless, but soon exhaustion overtook me, "I wonder what Mexican prison is like?" I whispered as I fell fast asleep listening to the soothing sound of the powerful ocean.

I had slept for a few hours when the marine layer cleared and things warmed up. I was hot and I threw off the quilt and went inside the house looking for Enzo, but he was nowhere to be found. I opened the front door and saw that the car was still there, but still no sign of Enzo. Had I been abandoned?

I was alone in a strange country and I didn't speak the language; I didn't even know what town I was in! Anxious thoughts quickly raced through my mind. Maybe he had been arrested! Could it be that the police hadn't found me on the bottom terrace? If that were the case, I wasn't about to stick around and wait to find out; I had to get out of there before someone took the car! I looked for the keys and wasn't surprised when I didn't find them. I dashed outside and tried the car door and it was unlocked. "Great, at least I don't have to break the window."

I laid down on the floor of the car and reached under the dash. "I saw Vic do this," I said, as I pulled out the wires. "I can hotwire a car, it's not that difficult," I told myself trying to bolster my courage. "Come on, come on, Penelope, which wires did he touch together? I hope I don't catch the thing on fire!"

Suddenly I heard a man's voice, "Lose something?" he asked.

I jumped and quickly realized that it was Enzo, "Oh, you startled me," I said, as I shoved the wires back under the dash. "I was just looking for my earring." I pulled the earring from my ear and held it in my hand, "Here it is!" I cheerfully declared as I got to my feet.

"I went to the restaurant down the lane, hope you like Mexican," Enzo chuckled.

"Sure, Mexican's fine, when in Rome, do as the Romans," I said, and took a breath of relief.

Enzo and I went to the back of the villa and sat on the terrace. "Oh, I called Emily from the restaurant," he said, as he opened the bag containing the food, "something came up and she isn't planning to come here until sometime next month. She offered to let us to stay as long as we want to."

Enzo was lying; the place obviously didn't belong to Emily. What was he up to? How long did he plan to keep me here? "We can't stay too long, you've got to get the restaurant going," I reminded him.

Enzo looked at me and grinned, "I think it's pretty clear that Ross isn't going to buy in, so I'll have to call on some other investors. I may not be able to arrange a meeting for a few weeks, so in the meantime, let's forget about business and enjoy ourselves."

I pretended to be pleased, but I wasn't; I felt vulnerable and unsure, I was completely dependent on Enzo, a man who had broken into the villa and lied to me. There was definitely something wrong with this picture and I wondered just how bad the situation really was.

"How do you know Ross?" I asked, fishing for information.

"Oh, unfortunately, I like to gamble," he said. "Ross and I have crossed swords a few times, but I always managed to pay up."

Now I at least knew what Enzo's problem was, he was a gambler; it explained why he had gone to a mobster like Ross for a loan, instead of to a bank. I didn't have much faith in him at this point, but still maintained a spark of hope. The man had played the Super Bowl, he obviously had discipline and determination; maybe he could pull it together and start the restaurant.

While it was true that Enzo was a shady character, working for him was the best opportunity that I was going to get. I couldn't work a legitimate job; after my first paycheck, Vic would show up. Enzo knew my situation and was willing to hide my identity; he offered to pay me well, and I would be able to afford a comfortable life. I knew it was a long shot, but I had to stick it out with him and hope for the best.

After lunch, Enzo went to the car and got our luggage, "Pick out the room you want," he told me.

I went upstairs and chose a bedroom at the front of the house with a very high bed; there was a little staircase to climb up onto it. When I sat up on the bed, I could see through the window. I had a clear view of the road and the front of the property, so I could see if someone came up on me.

"Wouldn't you rather have a room with an ocean view?" Enzo asked.

"No, I feel safer up on the high bed."

I unpacked my bikini and spent the rest of the day at the beach, swimming and laying in the sunshine, while, Enzo, busily went over paperwork.

The day went by quickly, I had just come out of the water when I saw Enzo waving and calling to me from the terrace. "Come on back and get dressed, we're going out for dinner," he shouted.

Enzo and I drove into the small village to a tiny restaurant called, La Plata. I was hesitant at first, the place looked shabby outside and I had heard so many stories about the bad food in Mexico. Enzo assured me that he had eaten there before and when we went inside, I was pleased to find that it was very clean.

By the time we finished dinner and got back to the villa, it was starting to get dark, I turned on a light switch, but it didn't work. It didn't take long to discover that there was no electricity.

"It'll just add to the atmosphere," Enzo stated as he lit a candelabrum.

"Yeah, sure it will, it'll make the spook show complete," I thought.

"Let's go out on the terrace," he suggested.

It was a cool night, but each of the terraces had a fire pit. Enzo lit a fire and we sat next to each other, enjoying the roaring ocean and the warmth of the fire.

After a short time, he reached over and gently took my hand, "I don't want you to worry Penelope, I'm not like Ross, I promise, I will never force myself on you." He smiled sweetly and then kissed my hand.

I looked into Enzo's eyes; this was the first time that I had ever really seen him. I could tell that he was sincere, his hands were strong and reassuring, there was definitely something special about him. I placed my other hand on top of his, "Thank you Enzo, you don't know how much I appreciate that," I told him … and I truly did.

Late that night, after we went inside, Enzo and I each lit a candelabrum and climbed up the long staircase to the bedrooms. He walked me to my room and followed me in, looking in the closets and behind the furniture. "Just checking for the boogeyman," he said laughingly. Then he whispered, "Have a good night's sleep," and he closed the door behind him.

I took a chair and propped it under the door handle and then climbed into bed; when I blew out the candles, it was pitch black. The villa was a scary place, but I managed to go to sleep, confident that no one could get into the room without awakening me.

The next morning, was the beginning of what would become our routine. Enzo and I went to the market to buy food and supplies for the day, and then we went on the beach. Each night, we sat on the terrace by the fire. It would have been a wonderful relaxing time, if we hadn't have broken into the place, I was always on edge, waiting for the next crisis to hit.

I wondered what would happen between Enzo and me. I didn't want a romantic relationship with him, or anyone else for that matter; another man would only complicate my life. What I wanted was a job, but it was clear that Enzo expected more and he was waiting patiently to get it. After what he had said about Ross, he didn't dare make a move on me, or it would blow his image and he truly wanted me to like him.

As each day passed, Enzo and I began to get to know each other; he was never cross or impatient, always pleasant and kind. That was a wonderful change for me, especially after enduring, Vic's, explosive unpredictable moods. Enzo was quick-witted and charming, he had a great personality and we spent much of our time laughing and joking. The two of us were completely compatible and I was growing fond of him.

Enzo and I usually sunned on the terrace on lounge chairs, but this particular day, we decided to spread blankets on the sandy beach. I was applying suntan oil on Enzo's bronzing back, and as I moved my hands over his silky skin I suddenly realized what I was holding, a strong muscular athlete. Women clamored for these men. I had always assumed that it was strictly for the money, but now I wondered if that was the only reason. I ran my hands across Enzo's broad shoulders, and then slicked up his powerful arms. I then moved down his back, covered his trim waist with the oil, and then his firm sturdy legs. This man had an incredible physique and was well-coordinated as well; maybe it hadn't been such a good idea to deny myself the pleasure of this beautiful well-developed body. "Why don't you roll over Enzo, and let me do your chest for you."

"I can't," he answered.

"What do you mean, you can't?"

"I'm embarrassed," he replied with a slight chuckle.

"Well why don't you roll over anyway and let me see what the problem is, I'm sure that I can help you with it."

Enzo turned over, he took me in his arms, laid me down and kissed me passionately, "It's about time you figured it out Penelope," he said breathlessly, "I'm in love with you."

Enzo kissed me all over my body, and then he untied the strings of my bikini with his teeth. He was on his knees, holding the bikini bottoms in his mouth and growling while he looked at me completely bare, my skin glistening in the sunshine. "This was worth the wait," he said as he tossed the bikini aside and climbed on top of me. Our bodies were hot and slick with oil and I swear that I could hear them sizzle. We made love on the beach with the sun beating on our naked bodies. The crashing waves sounded in my ears, and Enzo filled me up. "I love you Penelope, I love you, I love you!" he repeated over and over again. The sexual tension between us had been released and I had made Enzo happy.

Enzo was incredible to look at, and firm to touch. He was no slouch and had definitely gotten the job done, but his lovemaking was a far cry from Vic. I questioned what I had done; had taking our relationship to the next level been a mistake? I wondered if it would have an adverse effect on my job opportunity at the restaurant, but then I came to the conclusion that it couldn't hurt to be the one who was fucking the boss.

Later that night, while Enzo and I sat next to the fire, he announced that he had a confession to make. I tensed up and braced myself, "What next?"

"I'm the one that blew the deal with Ross that night," he said. "Ross told me that he was interested in you and he asked me to back off, but I wouldn't, I wanted you too bad. When I hired you to manage the restaurant, I knew that it would push him over the edge. That's why he acted so crazy, I was taunting him."

"Shame on you," I scolded.

"And that's not all," he went on, "I never woke Carrie up, I didn't tell her anything, I just left her there."

"That beautiful girl? You shouldn't have done that!" I was shocked.

"Carrie and I were together for three years, but she was nothing but a trophy to me; I didn't love her and she would have only stood in our way. I brought you here, Penelope, so that I could have you all to myself. I figured that with a little time, I could make you love me, and my plan worked!"

Enzo was very arrogant, and taking a lot for granted; I didn't love him, not even close. I also think that he expected me to be flattered at his confession but I wasn't; as a matter of fact, it had quite the opposite effect and I found it to be disturbing. It almost sounded obsessive, stealing me away and isolating me in Mexico. I assumed that he wasn't sincere about the job offer either, and that he had just been competing with Ross. How could I have been so stupid? I had fallen right into his hands. I should have stayed with Ross, I would have been much better off living at the Laguna house, but I left without a second thought. Enzo was a master manipulator!

I was freaking out and tried to talk myself down, "I could always be wrong, Enzo could still be a wonderful man, and maybe he really does love me. Give the guy a chance and it might be okay after all." And that's what I decided to do, give the relationship a chance.

After our day of sex on the beach, Enzo slept in the bed with me and I must admit that I felt protected having a strong man lying beside me. With the exception of sex being added, our daily routine remained the same; the market, the beach, the nightly fire. Enzo was still patient and caring; he never expressed a negative emotion toward me. I didn't see any meanness in him, and I was beginning to think that he truly was a kind and loving man. Despite our stressful circumstances, Enzo and I always had fun together, enjoying each other more and more. The only thing that bothered me about him, besides the obvious, was his exaggerated opinion of his lovemaking. He thought that he was the greatest and continually bragged about it. I wished that he would have just shut up and things would have been fine, but he wouldn't, and it was a real turnoff. I wondered what other women had told him, and assumed that they must have built him up too far. Or, maybe I was wrong and they really did think that he was phenomenal, but that could only be because they had never been with Vic. My body hungered for Vic, but being with him was far too dangerous and after all, a girl can't have everything.

One morning, I was awakened by the sound of a car pulling up in front of the villa. I sat up and looked out the window to see a long black limousine. There were three menacing men with big bellies slowly struggling to get out.

"Enzo, wake up, a black limo's here with three, fat Mexican guys!"

"Great," he responded, "it's the investors; they said that they might make it today. What time is it?" Enzo looked at his watch, "Oh my gosh, it's almost eleven o' clock! Hurry, get dressed!"

Enzo and I threw on our shorts and sandals and went downstairs to greet his guests. He opened the front door, and after they all said their hellos, Enzo introduced me as his wife. I reached out and shook the hand of each man and when I did, I felt a cold darkness, the presence of pure evil.

I didn't let on that I was uneasy and invited the men to have a seat. I was about to offer them a drink when, Enzo, pulled me aside, he slipped me a few dollars and told me to walk down the lane to the restaurant. "Don't come back, I'm afraid that they'll take you from me. I'll come and get you when it's over."

I took the money and started quickly walking away. What Enzo had said disturbed me, "I'll come and get you when it's over." What was he facing? I knew that these men were evil and I was concerned.

I kept briskly walking, and when I came to a cross street, the people near me either scurried away or stood frozen and stared. I wondered what it was about me that they found so shocking. Maybe they had never seen a redhead before. Could it be that they were actually that isolated?

I went into the restaurant and looked around; it was a nice place. There wasn't anyone there but the bartender, so I sat at the bar and ordered breakfast. The bartender, Jose, was a nice looking, young man and he spoke English well, so we began to have a nice chat. "What's with all the people on the street, running away from me or staring?" I asked.

"Pay no attention to them, they are just uneducated."

"Uneducated huh, strange is more like it," I commented.

"They do not know any better, just ignore them," he suggested. "How long are you staying at the resort?"

"I'm not staying at the resort; I'm at the end of the lane, at the villa there."

When I said that, the bartender paused for a moment, and then nervously asked, "You mean at the Villa de Muerte?"

"I don't know the name of it, it could be that villa."

"Are you sure that you are at the very end? The dead end?"

"That's right, the very end of the lane. What does Villa de, whatever you said, mean anyway?"

"Villa of Death," Jose grimly answered.

"That sounds terrible, why do they call it that?"

"A short time ago, there was a shootout there and eighteen men were killed. The people at Villa de Muerte are very dangerous and everyone is afraid, even the police won't go near."

I sat on the barstool for about five seconds, I was a little stunned, but with everything else that had happened to me, this wasn't that much of a shock. "Wouldn't ya know," I said shaking my head, "I'm staying at The

House of Death. Jose, give me a shot of Tequila, and make it the good stuff, a double."

I sat at the bar drinking, waiting for Enzo to come for me, and Jose did what all good bartenders do, he listened. He was intelligent and fun to talk to, a respectful cultured gentleman.

An hour went by, and Jose's shift was about to end, "I am sorry, but I am leaving in fifteen minutes," he told me.

I was drunk by this time, "You can't leave me Jose, no one else knows English around here! Who will I talk to? And what if Enzo gets killed and doesn't come for me? That could really happen you know; he is at the House of Death! I might be left here forever!"

"I will wait with you a little longer," Jose kindly agreed, and when his shift ended we sat at a table together.

"Let me buy you a drink," I offered, "how about something to eat, order anything you want." Jose ordered a meal and we enjoyed a few shots together.

Another hour passed, "I don't think that Enzo's coming; is there a place where I can rent a car?"

"There is no place, and you should not be driving, you have had too much drink. We wait a little longer, maybe your friend will show up. If he does not, you can get a room at the resort and I will see if cousin Emilio can drive you somewhere in the morning."

"That sounds like an ex...cellent plan Jose, you're very nice. Cheers!" I exclaimed, and we drank down a shot.

More time passed, Jose and I kept drinking and he started to get a little tipsy too. The mood lightened and the conversation began to get loose. We were laughing, joking with each other, and having a good time.

"How much do you weigh?" Jose suddenly asked me.

"It's not polite to ask a lady her weight," I replied, "but I really don't care if you ask me, because I'm not a lady," I laughed. "Why don't you try and guess?"

"Very well, stand up so I can look at you." I stood up. "It is hard to tell, just from looking," Jose stated as he got to his feet, "come here let me pick you up, then I will know."

Jose took hold of me and picked me up, "Be careful Jose, don't drop me," I slurred.

"I will not," he assured me, "I am strongest man in village!"

But Jose was a little more tipsy than he realized and he lost his balance. I started to scream and laugh, "Jose, put me down!" as he stumbled about with me in his arms.

Jose was laughing too, he backed up trying to regain his footing and bumped into a chair, then we lunged forward, hit a table and I landed right on top of it. "It looks like you are dessert!" Jose playfully announced.

Jose and I were laughing loudly and hugging when I looked up and saw Enzo standing next to us.

"She's dessert alright, but she's my dessert," Enzo gruffly stated as he pulled me away and picked me up.

"I was just about to give up on you Enzo," I told him. "Meet my new friend, Jose. Jose, this is Enzo, the Villa of Death guy," I slurred as Enzo carried me to the door. "Good-bye Jose."

Enzo kept carrying me, "I can walk," I complained, "I'm not that drunk."

"Yes, I know that you can walk, it's faster this way, just relax."

"Okay I'll relax," I said as I snuggled up to him, "I was afraid, I was afraid that something had happened and that you wouldn't come for me."

"Don't ever be afraid, I love you and we'll always be together, no matter what. Do you hear me? No matter what!"

"You know, you're very nice too," I said with a sigh.

When Enzo and I got back to the villa a grim feeling came over me; I was back at the Villa de Muerte, the House of Death. My mood changed immediately from relief to panic, "Villa de Muerte, that's what they call this place!" I shouted at Enzo. "Eighteen men were shot! I don't want to stay here anymore! And those guys today, they were creepy. I'm getting out of here!"

"Just relax, I know what really happened at this house, I was here when it went down; a misunderstanding, nothing more than target practice. The locals are so backward, don't pay any attention to what they said, they don't know what they're talking about."

Enzo had been in the shootout, that's all I heard! I couldn't stand anymore and I went ballistic, I cussed him out, calling him every name in the book while I stomped upstairs and started throwing my things into my backpack. "I'm through; I'm getting out of here if I have to walk all the way to the border!"

Enzo followed behind me, "Come on now babe," he said calmly, "quit being ridiculous, I told you it was nothing more than target practice. Now stop it, you know it's not safe for you to walk on the highway."

"Not safe huh? And living in the House of Death is?!" I shouted. I was out of control and when I tried to leave, Enzo stood in the doorway to stop me. "Get out of my way!" I screamed. But Enzo didn't get out of my way; he grabbed my arms and tried to hold me. It really pissed me off, "I said, get out of my way!!" When Enzo didn't release me, I broke free and punched him hard in the stomach.

He bent over from the blow, but still stayed in the doorway blocking me. A second later, he began to chuckle, "Come on now, settle down, let's talk about this, you don't have to hit me to get your point across."

"What are you laughing at, you creep?"

"I'm sorry babe, but you're just so damn cute when you're mad. I can't argue with you, it's like arguing with a precious little, cartoon character."

Enzo's remark interrupted my anger and stopped me dead in my tracks; I was deflated, it wasn't the reaction that I had expected.

"We don't have to stay here," he softly said, "if you want to leave, we'll go right now. Whatever you say, just calm down."

It wasn't long before we were in the car, headed for the border. I felt like crap and laid down in the seat, resting my head in Enzo's lap. "I'm sorry that I got so mean," I apologized.

"You weren't mean; believe me I know what mean is. Sit up for a minute." Enzo unbuckled his belt and unzipped his pants, then he showed me a scar on his abdomen. This is what my former wife, Lisa, did to me. She cut me with a knife and I had to hold my guts in with my hands. Like I said, you're like a precious little, cartoon character when you're angry, I could never get mad at you."

I had noticed the scar before and assumed that he had had some kind of surgery; I was shocked to hear that it had been a knife attack from his wife. No wonder he didn't think much of me punching him. "Did she go to jail?" I asked. "Is that why you got divorced?"

"No, I loved her too much to get her into trouble. I was being an asshole that day and figured that I deserved it. I told the doctor that it was a stranger that had attacked me. Everything was fine between Lisa and me for a long time after that. She didn't threaten to divorce me for another two years. But before she could file, she got very sick. I loved her and I didn't want the divorce, so I took care of her, hoping that I could change her mind. But Lisa was stubborn and she wouldn't, right to the end she still wanted the divorce. She suffered for about three weeks before she finally passed away. She didn't have the chance to divorce me, but she left me anyway.

"That's a tragic story Enzo. I'm so sorry that that happened to you."

"Yes it will always haunt me," Enzo sadly replied. "But let's not talk about it anymore; why don't you try to get some sleep."

I fell asleep in Enzo's lap, his gentle hand stroking my hair. When I woke up, he was lifting me out of the car. "Come on Penelope, we're here," he kindly said, we were at a hotel.

In the morning, Enzo left the room early, telling me that he had business to take care of. "Maybe now I'll see some progress with the restaurant," I hoped.

I got up and took a long hot shower. It seemed like a luxury to me; Enzo and I had been taking cold showers or heating water on the stove for a bath. After that, I took a walk around town and bought a sandwich at a deli; it felt great to be back in the United States. When Enzo returned, we went to a Laundromat together and washed our clothes. Even the Laundromat seemed like a luxury.

I had only brought a few things with me, just what I could fit into the small backpack. "You don't have anything to wear," Enzo noticed. "We'll go tomorrow and buy you some clothes."

The next day, Enzo took me to see his designer friend, Lee. "This guy has a store on Rodeo Drive, but his workshop isn't far from here," he explained. "He makes beautiful clothes, and some of it's casual, you should be able to get everything you need. But, before you meet him, I have to warn you, he'll come on to you. He's got a wife and a mistress, and the mistress has a child by him; but even so, he'll want you too, so don't fall for his line of crap. He'll say anything to get his way."

"Okay Enzo, don't worry, he sounds like a real scumbag."

"Yes, he's a scumbag, but a talented one."

When we got to the workshop, Enzo asked me to wait in the car while he went inside and talked to Lee. After a brief time, he came back out and opened the car door for me. "Come on now, I want you to meet him."

We entered the workshop together, and I was nearly overwhelmed by the stunning clothing hanging on the walls and racks and lying on the worktables.

Enzo introduced us, "Penelope, this is Lee."

Lee was sitting behind a large worktable covered with sequins pearls and silky fabrics. When he saw me, he got to his feet and walked around the table. He reached out and shook my hand, "It's a real pleasure to meet you, Penelope," he said with a charming smile.

"Pleasure to meet you too," I responded. "Enzo told me that you were talented and he wasn't exaggerating, you have some lovely things here." The clothes were obviously very pricy and I figured that a little flattery couldn't hurt the deal.

"I've got to leave for a while and take care of some business for Lee," Enzo told me. "You pick out whatever you want, and be sure to get something nice for evening." He gave me a kiss and drove away.

I turned my attention to Lee, "I don't even know where to begin," I said shyly.

"Why don't you let me make something special for you," Lee suggested, "this green will go perfectly with your hair and eyes." He held up a piece of soft fabric and brushed it against my cheek. "You just tell me what you want, whatever it is, I'll give it to you."

Enzo wasn't kidding, this guy was making his move right out the gate! "Thank you very much, but there are so many lovely things here, I'm sure that I won't have a problem finding everything I need."

I broke away from Lee and browsed through the clothing. I tried on a few things and when I asked Lee the prices, I almost fell over!

"Don't worry about the price," he told me, "Enzo is more than earning it today."

Another jolt, "What the hell was Enzo doing for this guy?" Whatever it was, I didn't want to know about it.

I tried to keep the conversation light, but Lee kept pressing me. Then he asked how I knew Enzo. "I really don't know him at all," I responded, "we just met a few weeks ago."

Lee got a concerned look on his face, "Don't you know anything about him?" he asked.

"Beside the fact that he played the Super Bowl, not much. He's been very nice to me and he's planning to open an excellent restaurant, it's going to be a fabulous place." I started to explain Enzo's plan for the restaurant, the big band music, etc., when Lee interrupted me.

"You sweet innocent thing!" he loudly blurted out. "There is no restaurant! The whole thing is just a scam! Enzo is selling guns to the Mexican Cartel! There's a hit out on him! It's not safe for you to be with the man, when they take him out, chances are, they'll hit you too! I can't stand by, do nothing and let you be killed. You better stay here with me, I'll take care of you and keep you safe."

Before I could respond, a Rolls Royce pulled up in front of the shop and interrupted. A blonde woman got out, toting a toddler. She complained about some bills and Lee reached into his pocket and counted out ten thousand dollars. After she received the money the woman got back in the car and left; I figured that she must have been the mistress.

Once she pulled away, Lee went on as though our conversation hadn't been interrupted. "Let me lock the place up for a few minutes and take you out of here. When Enzo comes back I'll just tell him that you took off and that I don't know where you went."

Even though Enzo had warned me about Lee, I was still a little taken back. I know that men can be ruthless when it comes to women, but this guy was the nastiest, telling me that Enzo was selling guns to the Mexican Cartel! It doesn't get any worse.

Lee's story was outrageous, but even so, he was offering to take care of me and protect me as well. It was my chance to get away from Enzo, if I wanted to. It was obvious that Lee was extremely generous with his mistress and chances were that I could be the next woman with a luxurious Rolls Royce, but I wasn't interested in being the latest addition to Lee's harem. And even though I didn't love Enzo, he was always so sweet and kind to me, I couldn't hurt him that way. I told Lee that I was doing just fine and staved off his advances until Enzo returned.

When Enzo did get back to the workshop, Lee acted as though nothing had happened between us, and so did I.

Enzo browsed through the clothing and picked out a few more things for me to try on and in the end; I walked out of there with a glamorous wardrobe.

After we left the warehouse, Enzo didn't go back to the hotel as I expected him to; he drove straight to a car rental place to trade the car for another one. While he was inside the office, I thought about what Lee had just told me; changing vehicles was definitely a red light, a tactic to avoid a hit. Lee had planted the seed of doubt.

When Enzo came out of the office, he was smiling and holding the keys to a Mercedes, "This is much nicer, don't you think?" he asked as we got inside. "I thought that you would enjoy a more luxurious car. And now we have one more stop to make before we go back to the hotel."

Enzo pulled into the parking lot of an adult store and coaxed me to go inside with him. He went through the shelves and picked out a few strange sex toys. He wanted me to choose something too, but I was uncomfortable even being there and was happy when we finally left.

Enzo could hardly wait to go to bed that night; he was anxious to try out all of his crazy new toys. I would have preferred a good hearty fuck to all of his rigmarole, but I tried to be patient and tolerate it. The unpleasant situation made me miss Vic all the more; he never needed any extra stimulation and either did I.

After the arduous night, I was hopeful the next day when Enzo wanted to show me the building where he planned to have the restaurant. I eagerly welcomed any sign of progress, and happily got into the car. The site wasn't far from the hotel, but I noticed myself fearfully flashing my eyes, looking for suspicious characters, a hit man perhaps?

After we arrived and went into the building, Enzo pointed out where he planned to put the bandstand and dance floor. "The tables will be placed around here, in this area, and we'll have the cash register and a counter with the stand for your greeting card display next to the planter."

I was touched, Enzo hadn't forgotten about my greeting cards and even had a place planned for the display. As usual, he was sweet and considerate. How could I doubt him?

"My investors will be here sometime tomorrow to check the site," he informed me. "If they like what they see, we're in business."

"The site's great, of course they'll like it," I said enthusiastically.

Enzo pulled me close and gave me a hug. "I won't let you down babe," he promised.

The next day, Enzo left the hotel for his meeting with the investors. When he came back, he was excited, "They went for the deal, now I just have to renew my permits and take care of a few things. Looks like it's all coming together."

For two days, Enzo was up early and out taking care of business. On the third day he announced that we had to leave the hotel, claiming that the place was booked and that our room had been reserved by another party. We packed up and moved to another hotel, not far away. Three days later, we moved again, then he exchanged the car.

Two weeks later, Enzo came into the room upset, "I can't believe it!" he exclaimed, "we spent too much time in Mexico and I missed the deadline for the liquor license. Now we have to find another location for the restaurant."

We left town, and the cycle began all over again, changing hotel rooms and cars. Lee's words were still ringing in my ears and finally I came out with it, "Enzo, you act like a man with a price on his head, please tell me the truth. Whatever it is, we can deal with it together. I just need to know what's really going on!"

"Sometimes people shouldn't know the truth," he said in reply. "Are you sure that you really want to hear it?"

"Yes, please tell me Enzo, I can handle it."

"Well you're right about one thing, we have been moving around because of a hit, but it's not what you think. I'm not the one with the contract out on him, it's you!"

"Me?!"

"I didn't want to scare you, that's why I hid it from you. I dropped the restaurant deal, the minute that I found out about it and got you the hell out of there. It's Vic, he wants revenge and until he's dealt with, we have to be cautious."

It wasn't hard for me to believe, Vic had been harboring a grudge against me ever since I had left him the first time. I was deathly afraid of Vic; he wasn't in his right mind; the drugs had twisted his brain and personality beyond recognition.

Then the guilt hit me and I felt horrible accusing Enzo. All of my suspicions and doubts, and here he had given up his dream of owning the restaurant, and put his life on the line to protect me. "Enzo I'm so sorry that I doubted you, I never will again," I apologized.

When I reached to give him a kiss, Enzo wrapped his arms around me and held me tight, "Don't worry about anything Penelope, I can handle Vic."

After that day, all of my doubts and reservations about Enzo had abated, and we were closer than ever. Yes, we were on the run, but being with Enzo was like a never ending date. He planned interesting things for us to do every day, gun shows, art fairs, anything and everything that was fun and entertaining; we were there. We stayed at luxurious hotels and when we weren't ordering room service in bed, we dined at fine restaurants. Always staying in a beach city, we spent a lot of time enjoying the sun and surf. Enzo definitely kept me entertained and happy, but there was always the tension of the hit looming over our heads, and I wondered if it would ever be over.

It was a few months later, when Enzo told me that the cash was getting low. He explained that he was going to make a deal, and was up early the next morning. "I'll be back tonight, don't wait up," he said. He kissed me good-bye and then went out the door.

I didn't hear from Enzo all day and it wasn't like him, he always called me to check in, and now it was nearly midnight and I still hadn't heard a word. Thinking the worst, I wanted to run, but if I did, we would never find each other again. There was nothing that I could do but wait, fearfully wait, dreading every minute that slowly passed by.

It was four o' clock in the morning when Enzo finally came bursting through the door with a large bag in his hand. Before I could speak, he opened it and began throwing money at me by the handfuls, "Look babe, it's raining money!"

"What'd ya do, rob a bank?" I asked, wondering if it was true.

"No," he answered, "I sold a yacht for a friend of mine, right here at the port, this is my commission.

"I wish you would have called, I was worried that something had happened to you."

"I'm sorry, but you had nothing to worry about, I was right here in town all day."

I didn't ask any more questions, it was obvious that Enzo was lying, if he had been in town all day, he would have called me several times like he always did. Wherever he had been, it was impossible for him to place a call.

I began to pick up the money, and put it back in the bag. It was all one hundred dollar bills, way too much money for a simple commission. I was hoping that Enzo hadn't done something illegal, but if he had, I really couldn't blame him, he was watching out for me. I decided to keep my mouth shut and act pleased.

Once the money was back in the bag, Enzo showered and climbed into bed with me. We had sex, but I found myself holding back, both in fear and doubt. As Enzo told me how much he loved me, I wondered who he really was.

Enzo and I slept until checkout time, when we got up, it was business as usual and we prepared to relocate. Enzo was in the bathroom shaving and I was ready to go. I pushed the bathroom door open a little, "Enzo, I'm going to the convenience store down the block, to pick up some lip balm, do you need anything?"

"No, I'm fine," he answered.

"I'll meet you at the car."

"Okay, I'll just be a few more minutes."

As I rode the elevator down to the lobby, I noticed that I had a full tube of lip balm in my purse. Since Enzo didn't need anything from the store, I decided to sit in the car and listen to music while I waited for him.

I was calmly enjoying soothing classical music when I noticed a crushed paper bag shoved between the driver's seat and the console. I decided to throw it in the trash, but when I picked it up, the bag looked familiar. I pulled out the folds and was distressed to read, La Plata; this bag was from the little restaurant in Mexico; Enzo had been at The Villa de Muerte!

I quickly glanced around the parking garage; Enzo wasn't anywhere in sight, so I decided to look for more evidence. I opened the trunk of the car, hoping with everything in me that I wouldn't find anything incriminating, but when I searched, I found ammo cans, marked M60, 7.62. This was no game, the M60 is a powerful hand-held, machine gun, a serious weapon. I slammed the trunk shut and got in the car before Enzo could see me.

I felt sick inside, the horrible truth had been revealed and I had to face it, Enzo was selling guns to the Mexican Cartel. There was no other explanation. Lee had been telling me the truth and he was genuinely trying to help me! I had made a dreadful mistake!

Enzo couldn't find out what I knew, I had to act natural and I struggled to pull myself together. "What the hell is wrong with me?" I questioned. "How do I always find myself in these terrible situations? Why can't I ever meet a good decent man? Why couldn't Enzo have been an honest football player, a businessman opening a restaurant like I thought he was?" This was too much for me to bear. I had left Vic, for all the good that it had done me, I was still getting into trouble with bad guys!

Vic … I began to think about him. Had Enzo been lying about him too?

How could he know that Vic had a contract out on me? I had never questioned it. I decided to call Wendy as soon as I had the chance, and try to find out the truth.

Once Enzo and I had checked into the new hotel and got settled, he went out to run an errand. This was my opportunity, and I walked to the nearest pay phone and called Wendy. I was happily surprised when she answered.

"Hi Wendy, it's me, Penelope," I announced, and then there was complete silence.

"Penelope, is it really you?" she finally asked in disbelief.

"Yes, it's me, I'm just wondering how you're doing."

"I can't believe it, it's really you!" Wendy began to cry, "No one could find a trace of you; we thought you were dead! I'm so happy to hear your voice. What happened, are you okay?"

"I'm fine, Wendy, how are things there with you and Vic?"

"Everything would be great if you would just come home, please Penelope come home! Vic blames himself; he knows that he drove you away. He's changed so much you wouldn't believe it; he's done everything that he promised you he would. He's completely off drugs and he goes every day to see that old black woman, Mama Mable, the prayer warrior and the two of them pray together for hours."

"That is great news Wendy, but what about all the other shit? What's going on with the Feds and the Ruffalos?"

"Good news there too," Wendy happily reported. "Vic completed his contracts with the Feds and then they went after the Ruffalos. Ruffalos fled the country, I think they're somewhere in Jamaica. They'll never be back, that's for sure, not with the charges that they're facing. Everything's peaceful around here now, Vic has changed so much, he's like he used to be, the Vic that we all knew and loved. If you come back home, things will be better than they ever were, I promise. Oh, Vic will be so thrilled when he finds out that you're alive! Please, come home!"

After hearing what Wendy had said, I felt a surge of joy flooding every part of my mind and body. I didn't have to ponder my decision, I was going home to the man that I loved. "Wendy, I'll be home today if you can come and get me, I'm in San Diego."

"Of course I will. I don't know how long it takes to get there, just tell me where to meet you!"

At that moment, the operator interrupted our call, wanting me to deposit more money. "Wendy, I'm out of change, I'll call you after I figure it out."

"You're with another asshole man, aren't you?"

"You know it!" I answered. "I'll make the break and let you know where to meet me. Don't tell Vic that you heard from me..." And with that, the operator cut us off.

I decided to tell Enzo that I was going to visit a girlfriend; he wasn't the jealous type and I didn't expect him to give me any trouble. As long as I didn't let him know that I was going to Vegas, I didn't think that he would suspect anything. But if Enzo saw Wendy's Nevada license plates he would figure it out, so I made up a story.

I got back to the hotel ahead of Enzo and started packing, I couldn't wait to see Vic. When Enzo did show up, I went into my act. "Enzo you won't believe what happened today. The day that you told me that we were almost out of money, I tried to get hold of my friend Wendy. I left my jewelry with her and I wanted it back so that we could sell it, but I couldn't reach her and just left her a message. I decided to try and call her again today, to tell her to forget about it and her roommate answered the phone. The roommate told me that Wendy had moved to Newport Beach and gave me her new phone number. I actually got hold of Wendy and she wants to come and pick me up so that we can spend a few days together! I can't believe that she's so close by! I'm so excited, it's been forever since we've seen each other! She's such a good friend."

Enzo reacted just the way that I expected him to, he was calm and gentle. "She certainly must be a good friend for you to trust her with your jewelry. But who exactly is she; does Vic or any of his people know her? It could be a setup."

"No, she's fine," I assured him, "I'll be perfectly safe, she's someone that I used to meet on the hiking trail, she doesn't know any of those people and they don't know about her."

I was hoping to call Wendy that second, and tell her to come and get me, but when I saw the look on Enzo's face, I knew that it wouldn't be that easy.

"Penelope," Enzo said sadly, "I can't believe that you want to take off like this; why, we've never spent a night apart. Why don't you postpone this for one day, that's all I ask, just one more night so that we can say good-bye."

"Enzo, I'm only going to be gone for two days, come on now, let's not make a big deal out of it."

"Well, it is a big deal to me," he said, "I need a little time to get used to the idea. Come on babe, I had plans for tonight. I wanted to take you out for a nice dinner, and then to a new nightclub. You can wear that sexy sequin dress that I got you from Lee. I can't let you go until I do ya real good, I want you so sexed up and satisfied that you won't even look at another man while you're gone."

A night out with Enzo was the last thing that I was interested in, but I was afraid to upset him, I didn't know what he was capable of. So, to keep him pacified, I decided to go along with him and give him just one more good time. Over dinner, Enzo tried to talk me out of going with Wendy, and then again at the nightclub, but I wouldn't budge. I did my best to be fun and charming and to act natural, but all I could think about was Vic. I was hoping that Enzo didn't suspect anything, but I couldn't be sure.

I dreaded going back to the hotel, I knew that I was in for a night of uncomfortable sex, that Enzo of course, would think was great. I prepared for the unpleasant act, but suddenly I began to feel nauseous. "I'm sorry Enzo, I feel sick, like I'm going to throw up."

"Don't worry about me," he said kindly, "I just hope you're alright. Is there anything that I can do to help you feel better?"

Enzo had no sooner finished his sentence, when I ran to the bathroom and vomited. I sat on the bathroom floor until I could stand, and then I cleaned myself up and climbed into bed. "I must have eaten something that didn't agree with me, I'm sure that I'll feel better now."

When Enzo and I began to kiss, I didn't feel better, I felt worse and had to run to the bathroom again. Enzo came in and held my hair, when the bout was over, he wiped my face with a damp washcloth and helped me back into bed. I got worse as the night went on, vomiting one time after another. I was in severe pain and dizzy, my head was pounding. The next morning, still no relief, there was no way that I could meet Wendy; my plan would have to wait until I was better.

There was no room service at the hotel, and I asked Enzo to walk to the restaurant next door and get me some chicken noodle soup. Enzo came back with chicken vegetable. "They don't have chicken noodle," he explained.

I slowly sipped the soup and was able to finish it, but minutes later I threw it back up and felt even worse, the vomiting gave me no relief. I didn't want to become dehydrated and asked Enzo if he would please go to the grocery store. "Enzo, I'd like to try saltines and ginger ale, would you mind going to the store for me?"

"Of course not," Enzo replied, "all I ever wanted to do was take care of you."

He bent down to kiss me and I put my hand on his chest and stopped him, "You don't want to catch this," but he was unconcerned and kissed me anyway.

Days passed, and I expected to snap out of it, but I didn't, I continued to get weaker. I was dizzy and shaky and could barely move from the bed to the bathroom. As soon as I would begin to get the slightest bit better and was able to eat soup, I was slammed with another horrific bout of vomiting. This went on for two weeks.

It was day fifteen. I had just finished a bowl of soup and was vomiting when blood came gushing out of my mouth. I collapsed on the bathroom floor, "Enzo, I'm dying, take me to the hospital!"

I looked into Enzo's eyes and I saw fear, not the kind of anxiety that one would expect to see in such an emergency, it was completely different, it was a fear that he had gone too far! I don't know how, but at that moment I could read his mind and I knew that he had been poisoning me!

"Now don't worry," Enzo said calmly as he sat me up, "you're not dying." He wiped the blood from my mouth, "It's just a broken blood vessel. The lady up the hall has the same thing, it's a flu that's going around, you'll start feeling better tomorrow."

My speech was slurred, "Please, take me to the hospital."

"Now you be a good girl," Enzo told me as he put me into bed, "wait just one more day, tomorrow you'll feel better, I promise."

I helplessly laid there watching Enzo, he unplugged the phone and placed it across the room from me, then he closed the heavy curtains on the windows and the room became dark, like a coffin.

He climbed into bed behind me and held me close. I was stiff with fear, my heart laboring, pounding loudly in my ears. This man was murdering me!

Suddenly, I remembered what Enzo had told me about his former wife Lisa, "She wanted to divorce me, but before she could file, she got sick…I took care of her, hoping that she would change her mind, but she didn't and she died." Lisa didn't change her mind, Lisa didn't change her mind and she died, and she died! I had better change my mind! "Enzo," I said as I struggled to turn toward him. "I've changed my mind, I don't want to go to Wendy's."

Enzo helped me turn toward him, he kissed me on the forehead, "Thank goodness," he said happily, "that's what I was hoping for."

"You've been so great, taking care of me," I went on, "I couldn't bear to be away from you for even one night. You were absolutely right, I shouldn't have been going anywhere without you."

"I know you'll get better now," Enzo confidently told me, "you just get some sleep, you'll see."

The next morning, Enzo left the room for a short time and came back with chicken noodle soup; after all this time, the restaurant now had chicken noodle. The clear broth and simple mild flavor wouldn't lend itself to conceal a poison. This was further confirmation that I was correct. I thanked Enzo for the soup, but claimed that I would eat it later. I wasn't about to take a chance, and when he wasn't looking I dumped it down the toilet.

For days, I ate nothing but saltines and drank ginger ale from sealed bottles. My strength was returning, and I knew that my suspicions were correct, Enzo was another obsessed man, one who would rather kill me than let me go. What was wrong with me? Why did I attract these strange men? The question tormented me, but at that moment I had more important things to do than to worry about the answer, so I got up and showered. "Enzo, you were right, I am feeling better and I would really like to get out of this room. Do you think that we could go to the restaurant together?"

"Of course we can," Enzo said happily, and then he got ready to go.

"We'll have to drive," I told him, "I know that it's only a short way, but I'm still a little weak."

Enzo agreed, and we drove the car to the restaurant. It had been nearly three weeks since I had had any real food and I could hardly wait to eat. I ordered a large meal and when I had finished it, I was still shaky, but strong enough to do what I had to do. "Enzo, I'm going to the ladies room, I'll be right back," I announced.

"I'll walk you there," he offered, "I don't want you falling down."

"Don't be silly," I told him, "I'll be fine."

I grabbed my purse and slowly walked toward the ladies room. There wasn't an exit in the restaurant that Enzo couldn't see from the table, so I made a break for it and ran through the kitchen. The cooks were shouting at me in a foreign language, waving knives and spoons, demanding that I get out. I pressed past them all, and burst through the door to the outside.

I ran for the car, quickly opened the door and glanced in the restaurant as I climbed inside. Enzo had spotted me; this was it, he had the other car key and I had to get out of there fast! I put my key in the ignition, and Enzo was already outside and running for me. I tried to start the car, but the ignition lock wouldn't release, "Oh God, oh God, please help me!" I pushed in harder and the damn key still wouldn't turn!

Enzo was unlocking the door when I pulled the steering wheel to the right and the ignition lock finally released! I raced the motor and shifted into reverse as Enzo opened the door and reached inside. He grabbed me by the shoulder and I backed up, knocking him off balance. He had a grip on my blouse and when I shifted into drive, he was still holding on to it. My blouse had buttons down the front, they all popped off from his tugging, but the damn thing didn't tear. Enzo had pulled me halfway out of the car and I was dragging him down the street!

I struggled to take off the blouse and once I got my right arm out, it whipped from my body. Enzo was holding the car door, but when I hit the gas and picked up speed, he was left lying in the street.

When I looked back, he had gotten to his feet and was running after me crying, "Penelope, Penelope!" He finally fell to his knees sobbing, holding my blouse to his face. I raced down the road until Enzo was just a speck in the rearview mirror. I was free and on my way to Vegas!

THE VIC SYNDROME

I got lost several times before I finally found the right highway. Hours went by, I was feeling faint and weak but I just kept on driving; I had to make it home to Vic. I can't remember how long it took before I reached Las Vegas, but it was dark when I turned down the long barren road leading to Vic's house. When I reached the steep driveway, I stopped the car and looked up at the stately home sitting atop the cliff. It had been both a paradise and a prison. I hesitated for a moment, but my love for Vic dismissed all caution and up the driveway I went.

When I reached the gate, I punched in the entry code, the gate opened and Vic came bursting from the house. I leapt from the car and into his arms while the stupid alarm went off, WHOAAAOOO… WHOAAAOOO … WHOAAAOOO! Yep, I was home alright.

Vic held me in a tight embrace, "I'm sorry baby, I'm so sorry, please forgive me," he whispered as he kissed me and cried. "I felt like I was going to die without ya, but I prayed and God sent you back to me."

I was never more relieved in my entire life than I was at that moment. I had escaped from Enzo and made it home. With Vic holding me in his arms, I knew that I was safe. I relaxed, and when I did, my knees buckled and I collapsed. "Baby, baby, what's wrong with you?" Vic asked as he held me up. "Do you need a doctor?"

"No Vic, all I need is you. Please, just take me upstairs." Vic picked me up and carried me up the stairs, he pulled off my jeans and panties and put me under the clean crisp sheets. I wanted Vic near me, "Vic please, hold me," I begged.

Vic quickly undressed, he climbed into bed and I felt his warm silky skin slide against me. He put his arms around me and asked, "Baby what happened to your blouse? Did somebody attack you?"

I started to answer, but was overwhelmed by exhaustion and immediately fell asleep.

For days, I slept, only waking when Vic came to bed or when Rosita brought me meals. As soon as I was finished eating, I couldn't keep my eyes open and I fell back to sleep again. Vic was worried, he wanted to call the doctor, but I didn't want him to. I didn't need a doctor exhausting me with tests and filling my body with drugs that might poison me more. I was sleeping and eating, that's all I needed, time to recover. And I did recover; when I got out of bed, it was over.

I was happy to find that Wendy was right, everything that she had told me was true, Vic was the Vic that we had all known and loved. He was off drugs and working hard to separate himself from the life of crime. Vic and I considered ourselves lucky to have another chance, and both of us were determined to make it work. I enjoyed every minute that I was with

Vic, and when we were apart, I missed him. I was happier than I could have ever hoped for.

Vic worked normal hours, no more all night deals. We had nice dinners together and then sat in the spa and enjoyed the view. Vic had never even been in the spa before this, he had always been too busy, but not anymore, he spent time relaxing and enjoying his life. At night, we laid in bed together and made plans for our future. Marriage was on the horizon and Vic and I had already begun to design our wedding rings with his jeweler. I wasn't pushing him, but as soon as he could make the break, we were going to sell the house and move away.

There wasn't any more of his craziness or quick-tempered fits and it wasn't long before other people noticed it too. Vic was soon back in the good graces of The Big Boss and he started working at the casino again. Vic assured me that it was a legitimate job, but I was still leery and wondered if he was really breaking people's bones in the basement of the casino.

I knew that it would take time before Vic and I could have a normal life; he had made dangerous enemies and I still had to be careful. So when my case against my former slumlord, John Stevenson, went to court, I was in a very precarious position. My attorney, Daniel Krieger, and I had been trying to settle, but Stevenson's insurance company refused to pay me anything. Daniel had taken my case on a contingency and had already invested a sizeable sum. He had never gone to trial before, but that was all that he could do to recover his losses.

When I told Vic about it, I wasn't surprised when he stood firmly against it, "It's just too dangerous," he insisted. "I can't get away right now and there's no way that you're going alone."

"Vic I have to go. Daniel has invested a lot of money and this is the only way for him to get it back. And besides that, it's the right thing to do; that landlord should pay for what he did, there's no telling how many other people he's hurt. And with all the evidence that we have against that man, we can't possibly lose."

"So you have to go because your little buddy Daniel will lose some money; well ain't that too bad. And the two of youse can't lose the case, huh? Well the two of youse are goin' to lose, because you're not going!"

Vic and I went on and on, arguing about the court case, until I finally got tired of it and dropped the subject. I decided that I was going no matter what he thought, and planned to leave the next morning.

After Vic went to work, I packed my bags. Before I left for the airport, I wrote him a note with the phone number of the hotel where I would be staying. I knew that he would be angry and it really bothered me, but I went anyway. When I reached the hotel, I already had two messages from Vic, ranting and raving that I was having an affair with Daniel. I called him back immediately, but all we did was fight; he wouldn't listen to anything that I said, so eventually we hung up, still angry.

I tossed and turned all night; between court, and Vic being so upset with me, morning couldn't come soon enough. Finally, it was time to leave and Daniel came to pick me up. The minute that I greeted him, I realized that I had forgotten my earrings. "Daniel, come in for a minute," I apologized, "I need to put on my earrings." Daniel came into the room and I entered the bathroom and closed the door behind me. I was opening my jewelry box when I heard the phone ring. "Daniel, don't answer that!" I shouted through the door. But Daniel misunderstood, what he had heard was, "answer that" and he picked up the phone.

It was Vic of course, and he when he heard Daniel's voice, he went completely insane! Daniel was shaking, he quickly handed me the phone and I heard Vic threatening to come to town and kill him! Vic was no joke and I was afraid that he would really do it! I tried unsuccessfully to calm him down and finally I had to hang up on him. It was very unsettling, but Daniel and I couldn't be late for court.

Daniel was rattled. I didn't blame him, but I couldn't have much faith in him either and hoped that the insurance company would settle. I kept on right on hoping, until Daniel and I entered the courtroom, but it didn't happen. With all the evidence against the landlord, the case was a slam dunk and I couldn't understand how Stevenson's attorney's expected to win. That is, until things got started.

Before jury selection, the judge reviewed our evidence. The furnace had been repaired months before the defendant's expert witness had inspected it, and we had proof. But the judge wouldn't allow us to submit evidence from the repair company; he said that it implied that there was something wrong with the furnace. But there was something wrong with the furnace, and this proved it! I couldn't understand how the truth was inadmissible; it didn't make sense, and that's when I knew that there was something underhanded going on. My suspicions were confirmed when the judge blatantly disallowed all of our evidence. I was in shock; I thought that Daniel should have been able to do something about it, but he was busy watching the door, waiting for Vic to walk in and shoot him.

The trial went on anyway, and after the jury was selected, the first witness to take the stand was the defendant's expert witness, the paid liar. He testified that he had inspected the furnace and that it was in perfect working order. He further went on to say that he had duct taped the furnace vent, completely closing it off, and that there was still no carbon monoxide released into the house. This was an old floor furnace, where did he propose that the products of combustion went? I couldn't believe that he had so obviously committed perjury on the witness stand! I was waiting for the judge to do something, but he didn't.

Then it was Daniel's turn to question the witness, I expected him to tear the man apart, he had told so many lies. There couldn't have been one person on that jury that didn't know that a furnace had to be properly vented. We've all seen it on the news, every winter, people pulled from their homes, dead, because of carbon monoxide poisoning. But that isn't what happened; every time that Daniel asked a question of the witness, the defendant's attorneys would shout objections and the judge would uphold them. Daniel wasn't allowed to ask much more than the witnesses name and occupation. Defeated, he came back to the table and sat down.

"Don't worry Daniel," I tried to comfort him, "you'll do better next time."

The next witness was the slumlord, John Stevenson; he was well rehearsed and flatly read his script for his attorneys.

Now it was Daniel's turn again to cross examine, but the slumlord had a case of convenient amnesia, and he didn't recall anything. His attorneys were objecting to everything and finally Daniel gave up … another defeat.

The whole trial went from bad to worse, and with all of the legal rigmarole and witnesses testifying who were only marginally involved, we had been in court for days. Every night, I tried to get hold of Vic, but was unable to. I managed to reach Wendy, but she hadn't seen him either, and that was highly unusual. I didn't know what was going on and I was plenty worried. Where Vic was concerned, there was no way of knowing what to expect, I could only hope that he wasn't doing something foolish, or dangerous, or both.

Back in court, it was finally my turn to testify and I was anxious to get it over with. I got on the stand and told my story. I wasn't allowed to divulge any information regarding the condition of the furnace, but when I talked about the horrific attacks that I suffered, and my struggles since the carbon monoxide poisoning, the jury was touched. When two of the women began to cry, the judge seemed uncomfortable and flustered and he quickly called a recess.

"Things have certainly taken a turn for the better," Daniel said optimistically, "the jury was very sympathetic. I was watching them and I don't see a one of them voting against you. John Stevenson was a very unlikable character and that works in our favor as well."

I looked at Daniel and shook my head, "I don't know, Daniel, the judge is against us; I think he'll find a way to stop the trial before the jury even has a chance to vote."

Sadly, I was correct; as soon as we were back in the courtroom, the judge actually reversed his own decision to accept our expert witness, and decided not let him testify. With no expert witness, it was all over. I had lost the case on a technicality. The defendant's attorneys pounced and demanded a judgment against me. Immediately, the judge charged me personally, with all of the attorney's fees and expenses and the court costs; in those two short minutes, I was financially ruined.

The jurors were appalled, they were rustling about and talking loudly to one another. Daniel rose to his feet, "This is a travesty of justice!" he began to shout at the judge. The judge was aghast and he ordered the bailiff to toss Daniel from the courtroom.

Daniel was right, it was a travesty of justice. I couldn't have been more righteous or had a better case, but the slumlord was a friend of the judge. We found out that night, when Daniel took me to the Country Club for dinner. There they were, the slumlord, his attorneys and the judge, toasting and celebrating their victory together.

On my way home from the disastrous trial, I didn't know what to expect. I still hadn't spoken to Vic, but at least he hadn't shown up at the courthouse or hotel and whacked Daniel either. When I arrived, I cautiously opened the front door and found Vic at home. He acted happy to see me and took me upstairs to make love, but it was weird, more like an examination. The man honestly believed that I was cheating on him!

I tried to tell Vic that nothing had happened between Daniel and me, but he just wouldn't believe it. "I still think you done it," he said "but I still want ya anyway." That was the only response that I ever got from him, and it never changed, he simply refused to believe me.

As time went on, Vic became more and more tense. He started working long hours again, and coming home in the wee hours of the morning. I didn't see him much, and when I did, he was usually abrupt with me. It was rare to catch him in a good mood. All the signs were there, and I suspected that he was doing drugs again.

Things were rapidly falling apart. How I wished that I had listened to Vic and dropped the case. But I hadn't, I thought that I was doing the right thing, standing up to the slumlord, helping Daniel out, and getting a few bucks for my pain and suffering. I deserved it, but in the end, it had caused my financial ruin and the destruction of my cherished relationship with Vic. I kept hoping that he would come around, but things just continued to get worse. But there was one thing that I hung on to, Vic said that he still wanted me, and as long as he did, I planned to stick it out; I still loved the man.

Months later, Vic and I were invited to a party at the casino. Not only was I happy that we were finally going to do something fun together, I also thought that it would be a good opportunity for me to find out what was really going on. When we arrived at the party, I was surprised to see a lot of new faces. I didn't know many of the people and was happy when Wendy walked in. Wendy smiled and approached our table, but immediately, there was tension between her and Vic. Vic made it clear that he didn't want to deal with Wendy and he quickly excused himself and walked off with some of the boys.

"Wendy what's the matter?" I asked. "What's going on between you and Vic? Has he done something to you?"

Before Wendy could answer me, a cheap-looking blonde woman came walking into the banquet room and Wendy was livid. "I can't believe the nerve of that bitch, showing up here!" she said sharply and then got up and went after Vic. I could see the two of them across the room, and it was clear that they were having words. I didn't interfere, Wendy knew how to handle herself, she certainly didn't need any help from me, so I just waited to see what would happen.

The argument ended, and Wendy eventually came back to the table; she was flustered and took me aside to talk to me. "Penelope, I'm sorry to be the one to tell you this, but I think that you have the right to know. Vic was fucking that blonde bitch while you were away. I wouldn't have said anything, but I don't know if it's over, she keeps coming around."

I trusted Wendy; I knew that she was telling me the truth and I was completely devastated. I felt sick inside and didn't know what to do. I was inconsolable and Wendy became more and more furious. "Don't worry, Penelope, I'll take care of this problem!" she told me, and then stormed back into the banquet room. Wendy's eyes flashed angrily around the room and when she spotted the blonde slut, she grabbed her by the arm, spun her around and pounded her to the floor. "I told you to stay away from here, cunt!" she shouted. Wendy wasn't done yet, she dragged the woman by the hair, kicking and screaming, through the casino, and then threw her outside on her ass. All the men were laughing, including Vic. Wendy was one tough broad!

It was over within minutes, and Wendy quickly came back to check on me, "I hope that that makes you feel better," she said. And ya know what? It certainly did.

After the fight, Vic wanted to leave. He came and got me and we headed home. I couldn't stop crying and Vic knew why, "Alright, alright, I confess!" he crudely shouted at me. "But I didn't do nothing that you didn't do! You were fuckin' that attorney, so I had some fun of my own. Now quit crying, the bitch didn't mean nothin', I ain't even seen her since ya come home."

But I couldn't quit crying, "Vic I didn't have sex with my attorney, that's all he ever was, my attorney!"

"You're lying to me baby, you're just like the Rachet, he won't never confess nothin'; he ain't got no conscience either."

I kept right on crying. My heart was broken and I couldn't stop myself, I tried to, but I was hysterical. Vic pulled the car over and tried to comfort me, "It's okay baby, it's over, she ain't no threat to you. You know that you're the only woman I love."

When Vic reached for me I knocked his arm away, and then I went crazy on him. I pounded his chest crying and screaming, "I hate you! I hate you!"

Vic didn't handle it well and I thought that he was going to backhand me, but he didn't. He reached behind the seat and pulled out a baseball bat and then violently jumped out of the car, shouting. Vic began to beat the Cadillac with the bat; he bashed in the fenders and broke all the windows while I sat inside. Vic moved around the car viciously striking it with the bat, over and over again. It was terrifying listening to the sound of metal crashing and glass breaking. When Vic struck the radiator, steam began to billow out from under the hood. I wanted to run away, but the door was so badly dented that I couldn't push it open.

Vic's violent fit definitely did snap me out of my hysteria and I began to scream at him, "Vic! Stop! Stop it! You're killing my car!"

But Vic didn't stop; instead he jumped on the hood, waving the bat and screaming wildly like a madman, radiator steam swirling around him in a nightmarish scene. Vic looked at me through the broken windshield, his face was distorted and crazy; I wondered if he was going to break through and pound me next, but instead he began to strike the roof. With each swing he took, I could see the dent from inside the car.

The Cadillac had been beaten beyond recognition when Vic finally stopped, he was exhausted, panting and standing with the bat in his hand. I wondered what he would do next, and then he began to force open the driver's door. I didn't know if he had completely lost his mind, and I slid away from him, reached into my purse and held tightly to my knife, hoping that I wouldn't have to use it.

Vic didn't say a word to me and simply shifted the battered car into drive. I don't know how, but the engine was still running, it sputtered a bit, but moved ahead and actually made it down the road and up the driveway to the house. Vic got out of the car and then he reached in and took my arm, "Come on baby, let's get in the house and don't worry about the car, I'll buy ya another one."

I went into the house with Vic. It was tense, but bearable and I got ready for bed. Vic wanted sex, of course, and I wasn't interested, but after what he had just done to the car, I was afraid to say no. My heart wasn't in it and Vic could tell. "What's going on? You act like you're just letting me do something to ya!"

With all that we had been through, this was the first time that I didn't desire Vic; he knew it, and he stopped. "I ain't gonna rape ya baby, you let me know when you feel better." And with that, he rolled over and went to sleep.

As far as I was concerned, Vic had done something unforgivable and I couldn't stay with him any longer. I had been through too much with him and I couldn't take any more. I laid awake and tried to come up with a plan to leave him. But the fact was, every time that I had left Vic it was a disaster, and now I had a huge judgment against me besides.

I agonized for hours, watching Vic peacefully sleeping beside me, and slowly my anger began to subside. I tried to see things his way, "He was very upset that I left against his wishes," I reasoned. "He probably didn't know if I was even coming back. He made a natural assumption, finding Daniel in my room. Vic just made a mistake, he was upset and he made a mistake with that woman. She couldn't possibly mean anything to him; he wasn't at all concerned when Wendy beat her up and threw her out, he was actually laughing about it. Maybe I'm being too hard on him, at least he isn't doing drugs again. Vic has a strong conscience and he was feeling guilty, that must be why he was acting so distant and mean. Now that everything's out in the open, perhaps we can get back to normal."

Heaven help me, right or wrong, I loved the man and there was nothing that I could do about it. It was a force so powerful that I couldn't resist and I cuddled up and kissed him on the neck. Vic immediately rolled over and we fucked until morning.

Vic planned to stay home with me all day, but after breakfast and another good hearty, roll-in-the-hay, the phone rang. It was Tank, there was some kind of an emergency and Vic raced out the door. I wasn't upset that he had gone; frankly, I was glad to get some time to myself. Even though I had decided to stay with Vic, I knew that I could never trust him again. Things would never be the same between us, but there was still no escape for me. I loved Vic too much, more than I loved my very soul and I hated myself because of it.

NO TURNING BACK

I didn't hear from Vic all day, it was getting dark and I began to think that things were never going to get any better. I ate dinner alone, and at midnight, Vic still hadn't come home so I went to bed. I slept for a few hours, and when I woke up, Vic still wasn't there. I began to get angry and wondered if he was with the other woman. "This thing with Vic is never going to work out!" I said to myself as I paced back and forth across the bedroom floor. "I can't trust him anymore! I have to know what's going on!" Then the phone rang, "That's probably Wendy calling to tell me that Vic's with that bleached blonde!" I shouted angrily.

But it wasn't Wendy, it was Vic and he was frantic! "Baby, don't ask me no questions, just get in the safe room and don't open the door for no one but me!"

"Vic what's going on?"

"Baby can't you ever do anything I say? Didn't I just fuckin' tell you not to ask me no questions?"

I knew that this was a serious situation and I didn't care how mad Vic got at me for questioning him; I had to know what was happening. "Vic you tell me what's wrong, I have the right to know."

"Okay baby, I was just trying to protect ya so you don't freak out and get all panicky. But you wanna be a bitch, I'll tell ya all about it. I'm at war with an outlaw motorcycle gang, the muthafuckas are trying to muscle in on my territory. You're the only thing that matters to me and, THEY'RE COMING FOR YA BABY!! Now get in the fuckin' safe room and wait for me! I love ya and I'm on my way. And then the phone went dead.

Now I knew what was going on, the whole awful truth. Vic was dealing drugs again, this time he was caught in a drug war and the enemy was coming for me! I dropped the phone and ran down stairs into the safe-room and barred the door. I was shaking from head to toe, so I sat down and pulled a blanket around me. As I sat there, I listened, hoping that Vic would make it home before the bikers got there. I knew that if I was captured, I would be gang raped, beaten and maybe even killed.

There was a clock on the wall, and I watched the second hand moving, tick, tick, tick, tick, each second seemed an eternity! I looked around the room; there were weapons hanging on the walls, and rations and supplies, on the shelves. I couldn't just sit there and wait for Vic to come and save me; I had to be ready in case someone broke through the door. I stood up, pulled a Mac-10 from the wall and then I sat there, waiting to shoot anyone who broke in.

Holding the automatic weapon, I felt better for a few minutes, but the tick, tick, tick of the second hand was taunting me, Vic's not going to make it! Vic's not going to make it! They'll kill him before he gets here! My mind was going wild and the walls began to close in on me! I talked to myself to try and calm down, "You're in a safe-room, no one can get you in here." But then I thought about fire; if the bikers burned the house down, I would be trapped and suffer a torturous death! That was it! Something clicked inside me and I jumped up and unbarred the door. I ran to the storage room and found a large hiking backpack and then loaded it with what I needed from the safe room. When I was packed, I ran upstairs and dressed in black jeans, boots and my leather riding jacket. I tied up my hair and put it under a hat, then I took the little Beretta from my night table and slid it in my back pocket. I quickly pawed through the clothes in my closet and pulled out my ermine fur, then I ran back downstairs and shoved it into the backpack.

Fight or flight, whichever way it went, I was ready. Holding the Mac-10 in my hand, I opened the front door and cautiously stepped outside. I looked down the barren road to the highway. There was nothing but scrub brush, no place to hide if someone came down the road looking for me.

Then I thought about the car! Maybe it would still run! I ran back into the house, grabbed the car keys and when I turned the key in the ignition, the car started! I couldn't believe it! Things were going great!

I had driven the car out the gate and down the driveway when the radiator began to steam again. Oh no! No! No! Not already! I had to take the car as far as it would go, hoping with everything in me that it would make it to the highway. But I had only gone a short distance, when I heard the sound of motorcycles roaring toward me. I looked through the radiator steam and was able to make out four men, riding abreast, completely blocking the road. I decided to drive the car through them and shoot my way out.

I had my finger on the trigger of the Mac-10, ready to fire and I stepped on the gas, but the car had had all that it could take, it sputtered and then stopped running. Danger was staring me straight in the face and I couldn't give up, I turned the steering wheel and managed to coast to the left side of the road and stop the car at an angle.

This was it! I had to move fast, I grabbed the Mac-10 and jumped out of the car and when I did, the dome light came on, and the bell started dinging, reminding me that I had left the keys in the ignition. With steam billowing from the radiator as well, I might as well have been standing under a flashing neon sign with an arrow pointing right at me! I closed the car door and the light went out, but the bell kept right on dinging. I couldn't let it throw me and I took cover behind the front fender. I rested my elbows on the car taking careful aim through the steam. I felt as though I was made of steel while I waited for the menacing foursome to get close. I wasn't going to miss.

"You think you're tough, the four of you, coming after a woman who's alone, shame on you," I whispered as I looked through the sights. "WELL YOU WEREN'T PREPARED FOR ME, YOU MUTHAFUCKAS!!! I held tight to the gun and pulled the trigger. Ratt, tatt, tatt, tatt, tatt, tatt, tatt!!! I shot in a straight line, across the road and then back again, there was no question, I had hit my targets! "YOU IDIOTS MADE IT EASY FOR ME, RIDING SIDE BY SIDE!!!"

One of the men fell immediately, and his bike quickly went into the ditch, across the street from the car. The other three rode past, but then wobbled and fell to the ground. I stayed behind the car and watched, none of the men were moving, so I grabbed my backpack and started across the street for the bike.

The man who was lying near the car was still, but when I walked past him, he slowly pulled out his gun, in a feeble attempt to shoot me. It was laughable; I merely stepped on his wrist and pulled the weapon from his grasp. "Come on," I sneered, "I knew better than that in the seventh grade."

The outlaw was enraged, "Fuck you, you fuckin' bitch!" he screamed at me, while he laid in the road.

"Oh really, fuck me? Well, fuck you, you pathetic piece of shit!" and I took aim and shot him in the shoulder, with his own gun.

After that, the man didn't move anymore and I ran for his bike, lying in the ditch. I tied my backpack to the sissy bar and shoved the outlaw's gun inside. I looked the bike over; it was a beauty and hadn't sustained much damage. I was pleased to find that it had an electric start, it made things much easier for me and I started it up. I kept gunning the engine and running up the side of the ditch, struggling to get out, but it was just too deep and narrow and I kept sliding back down. The only option I had, was to ride the bike back to the driveway where I knew that the pavement sloped down into the ditch.

It wasn't easy riding, the ditch was full of branches and debris from a recent storm, but somehow I managed to keep my balance and move ahead. I was alarmed when I got nearer the paved slope, the men were much closer than I had thought and I didn't know what they were capable of. But I saw no movement, and decided to go as fast as I could, get past

123

them, and get the hell out of there.

When I reached the slope, I gunned the engine and got out of the ditch, but when I turned the bike around, to head toward the highway, a shot cracked through the air and I felt it graze my cheek. It shocked me, but I didn't miss a beat, I ducked down against the tank and kept right on going. The outlaws continued to fire at me so I zigzagged to make myself a more difficult target, until I was out of range.

When I hit the highway, I was flying. I had to put a lot of miles between me and the trouble, and I wasn't wasting any time. I wouldn't have to hitch-hike, the bike was running great, and it could take me where I wanted to go!

When the sun rose, I looked in the rearview mirror to check where the bullet had grazed my face. It looked pretty bad and I was concerned that it would attract attention; I had to keep a low profile. Who knew who might be after me?

KORY

I was so wound up that I couldn't eat, I had to get to my destination just as fast as I could and it wasn't until evening that I finally stopped. I don't remember where I was, just that it was a very small town in the hills, with a gas station, bar and grill, and a post office. After I filled the gas tank, I went into the bar, ordered a drink and got some change for the phone. I tried to call Pat, but there was no answer and I didn't dare leave her a message. My next call was to Wendy, and when she realized that it was me, she slyly called me, Suzy.

Immediately, I realized that Vic was there and that she couldn't talk. "Okay Wendy, I'll make it quick, how is Vic handling this? Is he going to help me, or try to kill me like he promised he would if I ever left him again?"

"Yes, someone has definitely been called," she answered and then said, "By the way, how you doing on that diet? You really should start RUNNING, and keep on RUNNING that would be the best exercise for you!"

"Wendy get off the fuckin' phone and get in here!" I heard Vic shouting in the background.

"Well Suzie, I have to go now, is there anything that I can do for you?"

"Yes Wendy, please keep my sister, Pat, posted she'll know what to do."

"Okay, I can do that, I have her number," Wendy agreed, and then she hung up the phone.

I put the receiver on the hook and held on to it for a minute, then I rested my head against the phone, feeling the full weight of my situation. Vic wasn't going to help me, and even worse, he was so insane from drugs that he had actually called a hit man. If he had gone that far, I knew that he had the Feds involved as well. I was a loose end, I definitely knew too much. Without a doubt, the motorcycle club was hunting me down, and they had chapters all over the country. As if that weren't bad enough, I also had to avoid the police, for all I knew, there was a murder charge on my head. I was clearly at the end of my rope, but I lifted my head and walked across the room.

I smelled food cooking on the grill and with a knot in my stomach, I sat at the bar. I managed to find a place where I could sit with my back to the wall and still keep an eye on the bike. I felt comfortable there and decided to order a meal.

While I was waiting for the food to be prepared, I got a pen and paper from the bartender and wrote a note to Pat ...

Dear Pat,

I'm writing to let you know that I'm on the run. I've shot four men, members of an outlaw motorcycle club. It was self-defense, but I doubt that the truth matters much right now. Things are chaotic, I'm certain that a hit man is on my trail and probably the FBI as well.

I'm headed for a safe place; you know that I can survive. I'll see you when it's over.

Love,
Sissy

I hoped that Pat would understand what I was telling her, and when I had finished writing, I walked next door to the post office and mailed the note.

125

When I got back to the bar, the place was beginning to fill up. They were a rough-looking bunch and as each new person entered, I carefully sized them up.

Everything seemed fine, but I got tense when I heard a motorcycle approaching. The driver pulled alongside my bike and parked. He wasn't flying colors and I didn't think that he was after me, but just to be on the safe side, I discretely pulled the Beretta from the back pocket of my jeans and moved it to my jacket pocket. Keeping my hand on my weapon, I watched the biker get off of his bike, and then walk into the shadowy bar. He was a handsome young man, tall, well-built and wearing leather chaps and boots. His long dark hair was tied back in a ponytail. The young man looked around the bar, as if he was searching for someone, and then came and sat next to me.

"Hello," he greeted me with a smile. "I'm looking for the owner of the bike outside, and you're the only one in the place that looks like you've been ridin'. Your ol' man in the can?"

"Maybe he is, and maybe he isn't; what interest you have in the bike?" I asked defensively.

"The saddlebags, I've been looking all over for some like that, I was wondering if he'd sell 'em to me."

"They aren't for sale," I said abruptly, hoping that he would go away, but he didn't, he sat there and waited for my ol' man to come out of the restroom.

"What happened to your cheek?" he asked.

I sharply glanced at the roughshod kid, intending to give him another harsh answer, until I saw the look on his face, he seemed to genuinely care and I softened a bit. "Thanks for your concern," I told him, "but it's nothing, just a scratch."

"Yeah, just a scratch, that's what my mother used to say, after my stepfather beat the shit out of her."

"Well there isn't any ol' man, I'm alone," I confessed.

"So what happened to ya?"

"Somebody took a shot at me," I said sarcastically.

"Well if you don't want to tell me, just say so."

"Seems to me that you're a little wet behind the ears, so let me educate you. Don't ask questions; if somebody wants you to know something, they'll tell ya."

"You're right, I'm sorry," the young man apologized, "but after what my mom went through, I can't ignore it when I see a woman who's been hurt."

"I'm sorry too, you seem like a nice kid; I'm just a little on edge."

"I'm sure you've got good reason to be on edge, you definitely look like trouble," he said with a grin. "I suppose that I should be more concerned, about whoever was stupid enough to tangle with you!"

Then I started laughing, "Actually, that's not far from the truth."

At that moment, the bartender interrupted our conversation. He placed a plate of food in front of me, and the kid paid for it before I could even get my wallet. I tried to stop him, but he insisted.

"Seems you're a little too quick on the draw for me," I said, then I let loose of my gun and reached to shake his hand, "thanks, I appreciate it."

"Nice to meet you Trouble," the young man said with a grin as he took my hand, "my name's Kory."

Even though we had gotten off to a rough start, I liked Kory, were having a nice time together and I regretted that I wouldn't have the chance to get to know him better. But there was no reason that I couldn't enjoy the short time that we did have, and we shared a bottle of whiskey.

"I won't be in town much longer," Kory told me, "the crew and I will be heading on to Oregon soon."

"Oh, you work construction?"

"Yeah," he answered, "we shored up a bridge on the highway. The job is done and I just got paid, but that's not why I came in here, I have a special reason."

I was a little nervous about that comment; what special reason could anyone have for coming into this dive? Could it be that he actually was after me? I slipped my hand back in my pocket, "Why did you come in here?" I asked, dreading what the answer might be.

"To celebrate, today's my twenty-first birthday!" he happily announced.

"Well, Happy Birthday Kory!" I congratulated him, and gave him a birthday kiss. The kid kept trying to hang on to me, but I politely leaned away from him, and then poured us another shot of whiskey.

Kory and I toasted his birthday, and then I stood up and slammed the shot glass on the bar. "Well, it's time I hit the road," I announced, and then I gave him a tight hug and a firm pat on the back. "Take care of yourself, and good luck with the job."

"Good luck to you too, Trouble," Kory said, and then he walked me to the door. "I'd like to see you again, can I have your number?"

"I'd like to see you again too, but it's impossible," I told him, then I walked outside leaving Kory standing in the doorway.

He watched me for a minute or two, then went back into the bar, "Let's get this party going!" I heard him shout, "Drinks are on me!"

I smiled at the kid's generosity and then threw my leg over and straddled the bike. Man, was I beat, so before I started the engine, I sat there for a minute to muster up my strength and get my direction.

Kory wasn't far from the bar entrance, and in that short time, I heard a woman approach him, "Well, big boy, is that a roll of money in your pocket, or are you just happy to see me?"

I took a quick glance back to see who it was; she was a brassy woman that I had seen with another man, just minutes before. "She must be the town slut, looks like Kory's going to get lucky," I chuckled.

I grabbed the handlebars, and was just ready to start the bike when a man started shouting at Kory. I could hear everything clearly, he was the brassy woman's jealous boyfriend; she was antagonizing him and trying to start a fight. I paused a moment, hoping that it wasn't serious, but no such luck. The next thing I heard was Kory yelling and then some banging and slamming around!

I couldn't believe it! NO! NO! NO! NO! NO! I CAN'T GET INVOLVED IN THIS!!! I started the bike and tried to pull away, but I couldn't. "Penelope, just leave! Kory can take care of himself," I reasoned. But it did me no good, I just didn't have it in me; the kid had a kind heart and I had to make sure that he was alright before I could drive away.

I left the motor running and got off the bike; I pulled the outlaw-biker's big gun from my backpack, and then I looked inside the bar, hoping with everything in me that I could just walk away, but the situation was even worse than I had thought it would be. Kory was on the floor being dog-packed by five men, and while they all beat him, the brassy woman stood by watching, bright-eyed and smiling. She had accomplished her goal, men were fighting over her, and she was thoroughly enjoying it.

The whole thing made me furious, I had to intervene and I stepped inside the bar and fired three rounds into the ceiling. That big gun being shot indoors was like thunder and everyone froze, including Kory.

"Kory!" I shouted, "Get up and get the hell out of here!"

Kory was dazed, but he finally pulled himself together and ran out of the bar. He had to have the time to get his bearings and to get his bike started, so I stood at the doorway with the gun in my hand, "First fuck that moves; I drop you where you stand!"

No one moved a muscle or said a word, but I was already in a violent state, and when I remembered Parker, my anger raged against the brassy woman. It was she who had incited the violence against Kory, and it was a woman just like her, who had caused Parker's death.

"Hey you," I shouted at her.

When the woman realized that I was talking to her, I could see fear bore into her face. "Who, me?" she meekly asked.

"Yeah you, you fuckin' snake, you think it's fun watching someone get hurt? Well it's my turn to have some fun now, get down on the floor and slither to me on your belly!"

"What?" she asked.

"Say another word and the next shot goes in your head."

With that, the woman got down on her belly and began to wiggle her way across the floor.

"Now hiss and stick out your tongue, like the snake that you are," I demanded. The woman did as I told her, while the others stood by motionless.

When she had crossed the room, she stopped at my feet and I looked down at her. "Let's see if you think this is funny," I screamed and I kicked her in the face.

The men made a move toward me and I pointed the gun at them. "Hold it now boys, this woman is suffering from lackaasswhuppin and I'M" ... I kicked her ... "CHANGING" ... I kicked her again... "HER" ... I kicked her again ..."LIFE TODAY! You'll thank me for it later." I gave the cunt a few more hard kicks, for good measure, and was backing out the door when I heard sirens.

"Come on Trouble," Kory shouted, "the cops are coming!"

I jumped on my bike, and Kory and I pulled on the road and raced off together. He waved for me to follow him, and I did, I didn't know the area and he seemed my best option. I could only hope that Kory wasn't doing something foolish, this was a country town with barbed wire fencing lining the winding roads.

Kory and I raced over the hills, with the sheriff in hot pursuit. We were hitting high speeds, laying the bikes down and scraping the foot pegs on every turn of the winding roads. There was no way that a car could keep up with us, and we thought that we had left the sheriff behind. But this was his territory and when Kory and I came blasting over a hill, we saw the roadblock down below.

The sheriff was crouched behind his car with his gun drawn, he knew that I was armed and I feared that he would shoot me down, as soon as I was in range. Suddenly, Kory made a quick turn off the road through a break in the barbed wire fence. I barely made the turn, but I was close behind Kory when we raced down a cow trail, back onto another road, and then pulled into an old motel. I followed him through the parking lot, behind the motel, and into a wooded area where we went down a dried creek bed, and then under some overgrown brush. "Okay, now shut the bikes off and be quiet," Kory instructed, and we did. I wondered if I had made a mistake, but it was too late to change my mind now.

Immediately, the sheriff and his deputy pulled into the motel, they were so close that we could hear them talking.

"I'm certain that they came in here," the deputy said. "I'm going to get out and have a look around." The deputy got out of the car with his flashlight, and searched around the motel.

"Come on Wayne," the sheriff complained, "they're not here."

Deputy Wayne scratched his head, "I know I'm right, just give me a minute, I'm going to take a quick look out back."

Deputy Wayne was coming our way; he was right on top of us and Kory and I held our breath as he walked back and forth, flashing his light. I could see his shiny shoes and hear the dried grass crunching beneath his feet with each step he took. I don't know how, but the man didn't find us and he finally gave up and walked away. "Well, if they were here, they're gone now," he admitted in defeat.

"Don't worry about it Wayne," the sheriff said, "we'll find 'em, they've probably headed out to, Farmer's Road." And with that, the Sheriff pulled away, lights flashing and sirens wailing.

"Phew, that was a close one," I said. "But what do we do now?"

"Don't worry," Kory told me, "I've got a room here, all we have to do is wait 'til things die down and then go inside."

"Okay, but what about the manager?"

"He's nothing but an old drunk, I'm sure he's passed out by now," Kory assured me. "I've been staying here for awhile, I know him; he's not going to do anything."

"Okay, if you think it's safe, I sure could use some shut-eye."

Kory and I waited until things were quiet, before we decided to make our move to the room. We didn't dare start the noisy motorcycles, we had to push them out, over the bumpy creek-bed and up the incline. I was already exhausted and the bike was so heavy that I was wondering how I was going to make it, when Kory suggested that we work together. "We'll get you out first and then come back and get my bike."

"Kory, you're a genius!"

Kory and I pushed my bike out of the creek bed and to the back of the motel, then he gave me his room key and told me to see if the coast was clear.

I crept out from behind the building and looked around the area, all was quiet. I found Kory's room, cautiously unlocked the door and then signaled to him. Kory quickly pushed the motorcycle down the sidewalk and into the room. Once that was done, we went back for Kory's bike and managed to get it too, without incident.

Once we were both inside, I closed and latched the door and then I leaned with my back against it, "What a relief," I sighed.

"Yeah Trouble, we made it, heh, heh, heh, Bonnie and Clyde!" Kory was elated, he picked me up and twirled me around, and we reveled in our victory.

But then it was time to relax and I sat down and put my head on the desk, "I really need a shower, but why don't you go first, just let me sit here for a minute."

"That's fine with me, Trouble, I'll get in right now."

Kory took a long shower, singing and scrubbing away, there was no question in my mind, he was definitely planning on getting laid. This guy was only twenty-one years old and had so much testosterone that I could taste it in the air. I doubted that he rarely thought of anything else but sex.

Here I was, alone in another motel room, with yet, another man. How had this happened to me again? How was I going to handle it? As far as I was concerned, Kory was only a kid, he hadn't had the years of experience that it takes for a man to become a good lover. And I wasn't at all in the mood to pretend that I was enjoying an inexperienced kid sweating all over me while he awkwardly humped me. But that's how it usually is with men, you have to take 'em as you find 'em, you can't tell them anything.

Kory finally finished showering, the door opened and he came strutting out of the bathroom, wearing pajama bottoms that loosely hung on his slender hips, and he looked adorable. I smiled as he approached me and handed me his pajama top, "Here Trouble," he said, "you can wear this if you want to, it's clean."

I kindly accepted the pajama top and got my toiletries from my pack while Kory stood in front of the mirror and combed his long hair. He placed the comb at the top of his head and then ripped down. "Kory, stop it, you can't just tear through your hair like that. Here give me the comb, let me show you."

I sat Kory down in the chair and began to comb through his long dark hair. "This is how you do it, you start at the ends and gently work your way up." His hair was a knotted mess and when I had combed it out, Kory took my hand and pulled me down in his lap. He leaned me back in his arms and kissed me, then he ran his fingers through my tangled hair and made a fist. He looked me in the eyes and said passionately, "I bet there ain't nothing else in this whole wide world that's as wild as you are Trouble," then he pulled me close and kissed me again.

I put my hand on his chest, "Come on now Kory, I'm dirty, let me get in the shower."

"No, don't take a shower, I want you to taste strong, just the way you are, sweaty and dirty."

"I'm not into that, I want to get the road grime off of me, now let me up."

Kory released me, "Yeoweee!" he hollered and then slapped me on the bottom as I walked away; he was a real handful.

When I finally got in the shower, the hot water felt wonderful on my sore tired muscles. I took my time, hoping that Kory would fall asleep.

Once I was finished, I put on the pajama top and listened at the door. I didn't hear any movement and figured that he had drifted off. I quietly opened the bathroom door, but when I walked into the bedroom, there he was, lying on top of the sheets, completely bare. His long hair cascading on the pillows and his beautiful muscular body glistening in the light. He was absolutely breath-taking, like a classic painting by one of the old masters.

I was a little surprised when I saw him lying there, and I took a step back.

Kory looked at me and smiled, "Teach me Trouble," he said, "I'll do everything you want."

I hesitated for a moment; this wasn't at all the unpleasant experience that I had expected. This was actually a chance for me to get everything that I had ever wanted from a man in the bedroom. I didn't have to pretend, I didn't have to do anything that I didn't want to do. This man actually wanted me to teach him, and he was definitely going to get his wish.

"Okay Kory," I agreed, "it would benefit all woman kind to have another good lay in the world." And with that, I crawled into bed with the eager learner to teach him how to please a woman. And he did please me, he did it all, just like he said he would, everything that I wanted and more, and the lesson lasted for hours.

Kory finally fell asleep and so did I, but I was restless an uneasy, I felt trapped and I woke up before dawn. I didn't want to explain to him that I was leaving, and take a chance of having a scene, so I decided to get out before he woke up. I carefully slid out of the bed, got dressed and then quietly gathered my things. When I was ready to go, I opened the door and a cold gust of wind came bursting into the room. Kory began to stir, I stopped dead in my tracks and held my breath, but then he rolled over and settled back down, with a smile on his face. He was still asleep so I went ahead and pushed my bike outside, but before I closed the door, and went on my way, I took one last look at my beautiful student, "I'll never forget you Kory," I whispered quietly, with a tear in my eye, and then I turned away.

I couldn't let emotion deter me; it wouldn't be fair to Kory to bring him into my turbulent life and he was too young to know any better. I had to follow through with my plan and I determinedly pushed the motorcycle down the street, away from the motel. When I thought that I had gone far enough, I started the motor and the sound thundered through the quiet town. I had to hurry before the Sheriff heard me and I quickly hit the road. I don't remember how far I went before I was confident that I had escaped, but I do remember of loosening my white-knuckle grip on the handlebars.

SUGAR AND SNOW

I rode for miles through the rolling foothills, and then I headed into the mountains, climbing higher and higher, first on paved highways and then gravel roads. I pulled onto a rugged dirt road and I drove until it ended, at same place where Pat and I had stopped with the horses, so many years ago.

By this time, the bike was nearly out of gas and it was too big and cumbersome for me to ride on the deer trails. I had to get rid of it, and I slid it down a steep slope and under some brush where no one would find it.

Once the bike was well hidden, I took my backpack from the sissy bar and put it on my back, now I was on foot and I started the long difficult hike. Pat and I had notched trees to mark the way back to paradise, and when I reached a turn in the deer trail, I searched for the first notch. Nothing looked familiar, I couldn't find the notch and I felt panic trying to overtake me. I tried to stay calm and I stepped back to get a wider view of the area, when I did, my eyes locked on to a small tree that had sprouted up in front of a larger one. I looked between the two trees and there it was, the notch marking the way! I knocked down the small tree that was blocking the notch, and moved on. Secure that I was going in the right direction, I hiked until dark and then set up camp.

The next morning, I was out of water and I started on my way to find the stream. Hours passed, I had seen no sign of the stream and I was beginning to worry, I didn't remember of it being so far away and I was afraid that I might be lost. Hiking uphill and carrying the heavy pack was really kicking my ass, but I kept on going, forcing my weary body to keep moving ahead, but it was becoming more and more difficult. Another hour passed, there was still no sign of the stream and I was so dehydrated that I had stopped perspiring. My situation was bleak; I knew that I had to find water soon, and I kept on going, slowly walking up the steep grade. It wasn't much longer before I was unable to take another step. I wearily dropped my backpack on the ground and sat on a rock to rest. The birds were singing their happy songs but then suddenly, they all went silent. I looked up and searched the sky for a predator; I didn't see an eagle or a hawk, but I heard the faint sound of flowing water! The stream!

No, I didn't start running and jump into the water, like they do in the movies. I would have liked to, but I was just too worn out. Instead, I rested until I caught my breath and then I slowly hiked to the water's edge on my shaky legs. When I reached the stream, I dropped to my knees, laid down on my belly and I drank like I never had before. Now that I had water, the pressure was off; I rolled over on my back and looked at the beauty surrounding me. I had everything I needed and I was safe in the wilderness. I set up camp by the stream that night, and when the sun went down, I slept like a dead woman.

It had taken Pat, and me five days of hard riding on horseback to make it to the cave and I figured that it would take me at least twice that long. I wasn't in a hurry, I was enjoying the journey and with each step I took, I was leaving my troubles further behind. The trees, the fresh air and the mountain stream water were healing; I felt near my Creator and by the time I reached the cave, I had been rejuvenated.

The cave was a welcome sight, and would be my home for an undetermined time. I scouted the area, concerned that perhaps someone else may have discovered the paradise, but there was no sign that anyone else had ever been there, just Pat and me. The rock table and chairs that we had set up were still in place, as was the fire pit where we had cooked our meals. It made me smile when I thought about the fun that we had had there together.

I decided to go into the cave to see what it was like, and I slid through the narrow opening. I noticed that there had been a few animals using the cave since Pat and I had camped there, and I cleared out the nests and debris to make the cave my home. When I was finished cleaning, I began to unload the backpack.

The walls of the cave were jagged and uneven and made perfect hooks and shelving. I had brought a crossbow with me and a quiver of arrows; I unlashed them from the backpack and hung them on the wall. "I'm going for the rustic look," I said with a smile. Because Pat and I, had been in the cave during a rainstorm, I already knew where the water flowed through the cave, so I unrolled my sleeping bag and laid it in the perfect spot. Next, I pulled out my gorgeous, white ermine fur; it was a status symbol, made to wear with diamonds and a slinky sparkling, evening dress. Vic had paid a fortune for it, but now it would have a more practical use, with its heavy lining and hood, I would make good use of it in the wintertime.

As soon as camp was set up, I got right to work gathering firewood. My tools were limited, but even in my rush to leave Vic's house, I had done a good job selecting what to take with me. While I was gathering wood, I found a straight narrow branch, it was plenty sturdy and I whittled it into a spear; fish was on the menu for dinner that night.

The stream was brimming with active fish, the spear worked great and I had a fish within minutes. I built a small fire to cook my catch, and after the meal, I relaxed by the stream and gathered my thoughts, wondering how this dilemma would all play out. Once Pat got my note she would know what I was up against. She had a good head on her shoulders, and with Wendy feeding her information, she would investigate. As soon as it was safe, I knew that she would come for me.

As far as Vic, the crooked FBI agents, and the bikers were concerned, I knew that it was just a waiting game. I had been around outlaws for most of my life and I knew the way that things usually went. Bad guys tend to live from catastrophe to catastrophe, each one a serious issue that they are forced to contend with immediately. Their lives and freedom are often on the line and they are frequently killed, go to prison or disappear, never to be seen again. I was certain that I would become old news as soon as a new calamity hit, but I just didn't know how long it would take, and I could be living in the mountains alone for years.

The thing that concerned me most was a murder charge; there is no statute of limitation on murder, but even so, there were still a lot of ifs. If … I had actually killed the bikers; if … they had reported it to the police; and the biggest if of all, if … the police even gave a damn about an outlaw motorcycle club member being shot in a drug war. When it came down to it, I had good reason for shooting the men; it was clearly self-defense. But for now, I was happy and safe, and I retired for the night.

I felt at home in my mountain paradise, and each day I did something to make my living conditions more comfortable and safe. One day, I built a bed frame to get myself up off of the ground and another day, I fashioned a tree branch to block the cave opening. Winter was just around the corner and I had to prepare for the cold brutal months ahead. I was busy hunting, fishing and gathering every day. I didn't have time to think about the past and I didn't want to, but the one thing that I couldn't escape was the loneliness, it gnawed at me. I had no books, no radio or television, no one's voice to listen to, and no one to listen to me; I came to find that it was the cruelest blow of all.

Before long, the birds had migrated south and the icy cruel wind whipped through the rugged mountains; the dreaded winter was upon me. I knew that it was going to be difficult surviving the grueling cold months. I soon found that my body burned a lot of energy just keeping warm, and I had to eat more often.

In the wild, I was merely a part of the food chain; there were plenty of hungry predators who would love to make a meal of me, so I carried the Mac-10 for protection. But I did my hunting with the crossbow and retrieved my arrows. I couldn't run out of ammunition, I had to make everything last.

When a storm came through the high mountains, the snow could be blinding and I was forced to stay inside the cave until it passed. Being outside after dark was dangerous as well; the temperature dropped drastically when the sun went down, and with the days being shorter, I found myself spending many hours alone in the tiny cave, hours that wouldn't allow me to escape my thoughts. Thoughts like: How did I go from busting criminals, to running from the law myself? The answer was always the same, the men in my life. Even though I had brought it on myself by choosing these men, many times I had been pressured into being with them, all the way back to my biker friends, when I was in Junior High School.

What would my life have been like, if I had made different choices? Or would I have been alive at all? If I hadn't been poisoned by the furnace, would I still have gone with Vic? But the fact was that I had been poisoned, and I had no other choice. Or did I? Were there other options available to me that I hadn't taken the time to find? And Enzo, another disaster, another decision made under pressure. And what about Kory? I couldn't stay out of trouble even when I was already running from it! All of these experiences were now a part of me and I wasn't even sure what I had become. Was it all part of a master plan, orchestrated by a supreme being? And the big question, HOW DID I END UP HERE?!!

Wrestling with my thoughts was never easy, but somehow I managed to suffer through and was always elated when the sun came back out and I was released from the prison of my own mind.

Fortunately for me, it had been a mild winter and the storms never lasted for more than a few days at a time. According to my calculations, the worst months were behind me and I was expecting things to start warming up. Soon, I would be enjoying the warmth of spring. I even saw a few buds beginning to sprout on some of the trees, so when I saw dark storm clouds rolling in, I wasn't worried and expected that it would soon pass. As it turned out, I couldn't have been more wrong, the storm was vicious and turbulent, a blizzard, and the worst that I had endured. Day after miserable day the storm went on. The winds were so powerful that they uprooted trees and blew them against the cave, crashing and banging and terrifying me. The blizzard was relentless; it completely buried the cave and I didn't know if would be able to dig myself out through the snow and debris. I hadn't prepared for this and I soon ran out of food; another day, and another, without food; I could feel myself dwindling away. Would this storm ever end?! I was starving, and all I could do was wait it out. I tried to sleep, but the roaring thunder and the trees banging against the cave from the unrelenting winds were too disturbing. No sleep and no food, but at least I had water and firewood.

A storm always ends, and this one did as well. When the wind died down, the first thing that I had to do was to get out of the cave. I didn't know how deep I was buried and I started to dig myself out, pulling the snow inside and pushing it to the back of the cave. I kept the fire burning, and as I pushed it in, the snow melted and ran out of the cave, same as the rain always did. It was a great system. I dug and chipped away at the ice and snow, forming a tunnel that I could climb through. When my fingers and toes got numb, I went inside and warmed up, but quickly went back to work. When I could see sunlight through the snow, above my head, I knew that I was only a short distance from the surface. I slid back into the cave and retrieved my crossbow, then I went back up the tunnel and broke through! I was out! Yes it was a victory, but now it was time for the hunt.

In the past, I had never had to travel far to find game, I had always been successful hunting in the area surrounding the cave, but this time it was different. I don't know if the storm had driven the animals away or if it was me; I was weak and hungry, perhaps my judgment was impaired and I had missed the signs. But whatever the reason, I had to expand my hunting area and I didn't like it. I was terrified of getting lost, my usual landmarks had been buried in a thick blanket of snow and everything looked the same. In my impaired state, if I got lost, I could easily freeze to death before I would ever find my way back to the safety of the cave, but if I didn't find food, I would die anyway. That's what I was facing and I couldn't turn back, I had to keep on with the hunt.

I established new landmarks as I moved further into the wilderness; the shape of the mountains, the tallest trees and the boulders. Trudging through the heavy snow was nearly impossible and I walked and walked until I finally dropped, flat on my face. When I tried to get back up, I slipped and then started to tumble, I fell over a ledge and then I hit hard on an icy slope and began to slide down. I was slipping fast on a thick sheet of ice, head first, on my belly, there was nothing for me to grab hold of and I couldn't dig into the hard surface to stop myself or to even slow down. I was terrified that I would keep on sliding until I dropped over the escarpment, but I finally came to a stop. I was relieved that I hadn't dropped to my death, but when I lifted my head, I found myself staring straight into the face of a fierce growling animal.

I tried to stay calm and reach for my gun, but at my slightest movement the animal nearly bit my head off, she had me pinned. This animal looked like an Arctic Fox, I had never seen one in these parts before and I wondered how it had gotten here. Was it possible that this was a dog? I decided to try and talk to her, "It's okay puppy, you don't need to be afraid, I'm not going to hurt you," I said in the sweetest voice I could. I was surprised when the animal responded, so I kept on talking to her and she let me slowly move. I managed to get hold of my gun and when I pointed it at the animal's head, she stood there looking at me in a sweet desperate way, almost as if to tell me to get it over with. This animal was nothing but food to me, my salvation, but somehow I just couldn't bring myself to pull the trigger. I lowered the gun and dropped my face down in the snow in defeat.

If I wasn't going to eat her, perhaps I could make a friend of her, "Come here girl," I said, and I reached out my hand. The stark white dog stood her ground, but allowed me to sit up, and when I did, I saw a stiff frozen man lying on the ground behind her and I realized that she had been protecting her dead master. This dog was a stunning beauty, with thick white fur that sparkled in the sunlight, a valiant animal, brave and loyal, even beyond death, and she broke my heart.

I called to her again, "Come here, Sugar, come here girl," I pleaded, and I reached my hand out to her again. The regal dog held her position, she hesitated for a moment, but then she took a step forward and cautiously sniffed my hand. When I saw that she had accepted me, I stroked her cheek and that was all it took, the next thing I knew, she was in my arms and we were both crying. I kissed her on the head and she licked my face. Sugar was the first touch that I had experienced, for many long lonely months. I tightly held her in my arms, elated at the miracle of finding such a magnificent being in this lonely treacherous territory.

I ran my hands over Sugar's sparkling coat, petting her, and as I did, I looked her over to see if she had sustained any injury. She wasn't hurt, but her stomach was practically touching her backbone. Sugar hadn't eaten for a very long time, probably since the storm had begun.

I had to check out the dead man; perhaps he was someone who had been after me. When I tried to approach him, Sugar was uncomfortable, she allowed me to get close, but she growled when I tried to touch him. I noticed claw marks in the snow and ice surrounding the body, it was apparent that the dog had continually dug the man out, as the storm raged and the snow fell. I looked at Sugar and politely asked her for permission to touch the body, and that time, she allowed me to. I gently looked through the pockets of the dead man for identification. He wasn't the law, or anyone else that I thought would have been searching for me. He had a deer rifle and his driver's license was from a big city. I assumed that he was a greenhorn trying to hunt and had simply gotten caught in the storm.

I picked up his deer rifle and ammunition, "He won't be needing this anymore, and now it's time for me to get on with the hunt."

"Come on Sugar," I called to the dog, and then I tried to climb back up the slope and get out. But Sugar didn't come to me, instead she laid on the ground and watched me with sad eyes. I hoped that she wasn't going to try to stay behind with the dead man. I was taking her out of here, even if I had to force her.

Sugar patiently watched as I struggled to climb the slippery slope; it was almost as though she was watching a rerun and knew what the outcome would be. Sadly, I found that I couldn't climb out, no matter how hard I tried, so I looked for another way of escape. I found that the area where I had fallen, was shaped much like half of a funnel, and I was at the narrow bottom. Above the funnel half was a ledge, too high for me to reach and on the other side, a perilous drop. There was no way around, the ice-covered, funnel-shaped slope, no way down the towering cliff and no way for me to reach the ledge. Now I knew the grim truth, the man had died trying to escape the icy trap that I was now caught in!

I didn't have climbing tools, there were no spikes on the toes of my boots, and the ice was thick and hard as concrete. I tried for hours to carve notches in the unbreakable ice, and the more I worked the weaker I got. I made a little progress and when I tried to climb the "stairs" that I had carved, I was shaking and could barely pull myself up. I struggled desperately to climb and had made it up about six feet when a strong wind hit the funnel wall. I was barely clinging to the slippery ice and the wind knocked me off balance. I lost my grip and slid all the way back down, where I found myself laying against the dead body. I was mortified, but so weak that I couldn't even move away from him.

Suddenly, the sky darkened and with the wind, came snow, if I didn't move, the snow would soon cover over me, this would be my grave and it was alright with me. I was at the end, no food, no energy, and no strength, there was no fight left in me and I didn't care anymore. I stroked the face of the dead man, brushing the snow away. "I wonder what people will say when they find us here alone together?" I asked, then I put my arm over the cold frozen corpse and closed my eyes.

The struggle was over, and my body began to freeze. I felt as though I was floating and entering into a realm of perfect peace. Suddenly, I saw a bright lustrous figure standing on the other side of a sparkling river and I realized that it was, Grandma. Joy overwhelmed me and I tried to go to her, but she told me to stop. "Weezie, it's not your time, you haven't fulfilled your mission. I didn't raise any quitters, now you get up and fight for your life!"

Grandma began to fade into the distance and I felt something tugging on my pant leg; it was Sugar, and she didn't stop pulling me until I was well away from the dead body. Sugar started licking my face, her warm tongue revived me and I opened my eyes to see the lovely caring face of the valiant dog. I smiled at her and then she began pushing against me, trying to stir me into motion. Finally, I sat up and hugged my heroic new friend, "You did a good job Sugar, and now it's time that we get out of here!"

I felt courageous, but when I tried to get to my feet, I kept falling back down again, my body was finished and I couldn't go on. I had to have food, there was only one thing that I could do if I was to survive, and I unbuttoned the frozen man's coat and then his shirt. "You're already dead, I hope you don't mind," I said. "You're going to be eaten, one way or another, so it might as well be us." I took out my knife and cut into the flesh of another human being, and then I put it in my mouth. While I was chewing the frozen flesh, I cut off another piece and gave it to Sugar. I would have expected to be repulsed at what we were doing, but I wasn't. The meat tasted good and Sugar and I wolfed it down until we weren't hungry any more. When we were finished, I buttoned the shirt and coat of the frozen man and thanked him for saving our lives.

Sugar and I had done what we had to do to live, but food wasn't all that we needed. We still had to get out of the icy trap and we had to get out fast, it was a heavy snowfall and it would soon be dark. I tried in vain to find a way out, but it seemed that Sugar and I were in an inescapable trap. I didn't know what to do until Sugar started digging in the snow. Snow, it wasn't the problem, it was the answer, we could use it! Immediately, I started piling snow, under the ledge, Sugar was digging it toward me, while I packed it down. The more it snowed the faster we worked and the mound was getting higher. It looked like we might reach the ledge, but then the snow stopped falling. I continued working, scraping up every handful that I could and piled it on, but the ledge was still too far from my reach. "Sugar, we can't give up now! There has to be a way!" Then, I looked at the dead man lying on the ground. "I'm sorry fella, but we're going to need you one more time." I dragged the frozen body to our snow pile and I slid him all the way to the top and secured him there. Immediately, I climbed up his stiff frozen frame, hoping that I could reach the ledge, but it was still too far. I called Sugar, and she immediately responded, she ran up the snow pile, and then on top of the frozen man. I picked her up and hoisted her over my head. Sugar was able to get her front feet on the ledge, then she scratched with her back feet and pushed until she made it! Sugar stood on the ledge looking down at me and barking. "Okay girl, now you've got to help me. I held the rifle up over my head, "Sugar, grab the strap girl, grab the strap!" The dog was incredible, I was counting on her and she didn't let me down, she got a firm grip on the rifle's strap and when I pulled on it she dug in deep to keep her footing. Sugar was holding my full weight while I pulled myself up, and when I got my hand on the edge of the ledge, she grabbed my hood in her teeth and pulled until I was safely beside her. We had made it! Sugar barked and playfully jumped with glee and I laughed in both happiness and disbelief at the strength of the heroic dog. "Good girl

Sugar! Now let's go home."

Sugar and I, began to hike back to the cave and with both of us donning stark-white fur coats, we were nearly undetectable. We easily avoided predators and besides the strain of trudging through the deep snow, it proved to be an easy trip. When we arrived at the cave, we slid through the tunnel, I opened the door, and Sugar and I went inside. We were both worn out, so I stoked up the fire and didn't waste any time climbing into bed. Sugar snuggled up next to me and we fell asleep together, warm and happy to be alive.

The next morning, when the sun came up Sugar was wildly clawing at the door, trying to get out of the cave. "What's the matter girl, you have to poo?" I opened the cave door for her, and as soon as there was an opening large enough for her to fit through, she darted out, up through the tunnel and ran away. I went after her, desperately calling her, but she wouldn't come back to me. Sugar was gone, and I couldn't believe it! I went back to the cave, collapsed on my bed and cried; losing her was so painful that I couldn't even stand. I was lying there staring at the ceiling, feeling dead inside when it occurred to me that Sugar may have gone back to where I had found her! I stood up and was getting ready to make the hike back to the icy trap, when Sugar came bursting into the cave. She hadn't run away, she had been hunting and brought her kill home for both of us! I was elated at Sugar's return! "Good girl! Good girl Sugar!" I praised her.

Sugar smiled proudly as I prepared her kill for cooking. Then we sat together, watching the fire and smelling the aroma of the fresh meat. I pulled her close and stroked her shiny coat, she was my dog.

Sugar was a fierce warrior; she defended her territory and protected me from predators, but she also brought fun and laughter back into my life. On sunny days, we romped and played in the snow, she was excellent company and understood me well. With Sugar in my life, I was safe and I never went hungry; even on the stormy days, she hunted, nothing could deter her from her duty, she was truly a remarkable creature.

It wasn't much longer before winter was a thing of the past. The birds returned to the blue skies and the wild flowers were in bloom. The warm weather called for a change of wardrobe and I designed something that was both cool and practical. I tied small fur pieces together and made myself a loincloth that covered my bottom, (very important when sitting on hot rocks). Next, I fashioned a belt and holster for my gun, with a pouch for ammo and a sheath for my knife, then I slung it on my hips. I always carried my crossbow over one shoulder and my quiver of arrows over the other, so I had to protect my shoulders. I cut a slit in another fur piece and made myself a short little poncho. I'm certain that one would never see an outfit like mine in any fashion magazine, but it was functional and I was prepared for anything.

Now that the stress of surviving the winter was over, it was time to relax. Sugar and I splashed and played in the stream every day, and laid in the warm sunshine. At night, we sat by the campfire and gazed at the stars. We were wild creatures surviving by our wits and senses and enjoying the simple peaceful pleasures of primitive mountain life.

One morning, I felt adventurous and thought that it might be fun to do some exploring. Sugar and I had never hiked upstream to the higher elevations, so just before dawn, we started off on the new adventure. It proved to be a good time. Sugar was fascinated by the many frogs, she barked and bounced in the water playing with them in a comical show. I tromped through the water and was moving ahead, when suddenly I heard Sugar yipping. I quickly turned with my hand on my gun to see what calamity had befallen her, when Sugar ran past me in a panic, with a frog holding onto her face. The ferocious dog had met her match in the determined frog, and I laughed so hard that I could hardly contain myself.

Sugar finally got her composure and shook the frog back into the water, but she was embarrassed and tried to act like nothing had happened.

"What's the matter Sugar, the mean ol' frog kick your ass?" I gave her a hug and a pat and we happily went on our way.

After a few hours of hiking, we stopped for lunch and then continued to climb further up the stream. The terrain was getting rougher, with big boulders blocking our way. It was a challenge, but we were well rewarded when we reached the top and discovered an incredible waterfall flowing into a limpid pool. Sugar ran down in front of me and dove into the inviting water. I quickly stripped off my weapons and clothes and went in after her. The water felt like silk against my skin and I slowly swam around the pool enjoying every minute of it. Then, I climbed out and stood on a rock under the waterfall, "Look Sugar I'm taking a shower!" I laughed, and I let the water crash on my shoulders, in a refreshing massage. "I'm going to see how deep the pool is," I shouted to my four legged companion, and I dove from the rock, down deep into the water. I was swimming near the bottom, looking at a mysterious underwater world, when something shiny caught my eye. I wondered what it could be and I dove down deeper and managed to pick it up. When I reached the surface, I swam to the shore to get a closer look and realized that I had found a gold nugget!

"Sugar look, a gold nugget! And I bet there's more down there!" I put the nugget in my pouch, and then dove back into the pool and looked for more. I turned over a few rocks, and there it was, another nugget! "Sugar we're going to be rich!"

From that day on, Sugar and I hiked to the pool nearly every day and I dove and searched for gold. Scarcely a day went by, when I left empty handed; it was incredible to feel my sack of gold growing heavy!

As exciting as it was discovering gold, it was completely useless to me while living in the wilderness; I couldn't eat it and it offered no warmth or protection. But if I lived long enough to return to civilization, it would mean a fresh new start and I would definitely do things differently this time.

Now, I realized where I had gone wrong; I had been searching for the happy ending, struggling to achieve the dream of living happily ever after, and wrongly believing that I needed a man in order to accomplish it. Each time that I suffered the pain of a broken relationship, I had always comforted myself with the same old line, "Don't worry, you'll get another chance for love and happiness," as though my happiness depended on finding a man.

And it wasn't just me, it seemed that most everyone I met was on the same merry-go-round, either trying to get into a relationship, or trying to get out of one. All of them striving to find the perfect mate, who would enable them to live the dream of happily ever after.

It was a shame that I had to be driven into the wilderness to find my answer; ENJOY EVERY DAY, and that's what Sugar and I did, we enjoyed every day and lived the dream.

The spring, the summer, and the fall were paradise, but winter was a grueling undertaking, where survival seemed a mere roll of the dice. But with Sugar by my side, to protect and help me, the odds were in my favor.

When the air got crisp, I began to gather firewood and prepare what I needed to make it through the cold months. I had no way of knowing how long it would before it was safe for me to return to civilization, and I continued to watch the horizon, hoping to see, Pat, coming for me before the snow began to fall, and the pass would be impenetrable.

I worked hard and my stockpiles were full when the first storm came. Sugar and I retired to the cave and snuggled by the warm fire. "Well, this is it girl, the snow's come and we're here for the duration."

I climbed into my sleeping bag with Sugar by my side and we fell fast asleep. It was just before dawn when I was awakened by the distinctive yowl of hound dogs! "Sugar, somebody's got the hounds on our trail!" I quickly got up, threw on my fur and grabbed my gold and weapons. Sugar and I climbed to our vantage point and waited with the deer rifle. The sun was just rising in the east and I saw two bloodhounds come over the ridge with their noses to the ground. They both raised their heads and let out resounding excited, hound dog barks, as if to announce that they had found their prey!

Sugar got restless, she wanted to go after them and defend her territory, but I stopped her, "Shhh, Sugar settle down girl, be quiet, let me handle this." Sugar quietly barked under her breath and gave me a doubtful expression, but she trusted me and sat still and waited.

I had the dogs in my crosshairs, my finger was on the trigger and I nervously waited to see who would come up behind them, prepared to kill, but hoping that I wouldn't have to. With the roads impassable and the mountain trails frozen, I wondered who could have possibly forged their way through. I was worried and my heart was pounding hard. Moments later, I saw a familiar figure come over the ridge on horseback, it was Pat!

There were no words to express what I was feeling, so I said nothing at all, I simply stepped out from behind the boulder and walked toward my dear sister, with Sugar close by my side. Our loving smiles said it all; it was a joyous reunion, but we had no time for emotional displays, there was a storm on the horizon. When Sugar saw that I had accepted, Pat, and the hounds, she let down her guard and enjoyed the company of her new friends.

Pat was ponying an extra horse for me and she handed me the reins, "It's rough riding ahead," she said, "we better get moving."

I put my gold in the saddlebag and my boot in the stirrup, while Pat turned her horse around and headed back down the mountain trail. The dogs took the lead and I followed behind.

I was elated that, Pat, had come for me; it was what I had been waiting and hoping for. But now that it had actually come to pass, I began to have my doubts. Sugar and I were wild unruly animals, accustomed to doing as we pleased. We killed to survive, and I wondered if we would be able to conform to the rules and confines of civilization. It would clearly be my next challenge, and one that I was uncertain of attaining.

But whatever happened, I had a bag full of gold and a scripture in my heart;

"Guard your heart above all else, for it determines the course of your life."

King Solomon

This book was brought to you by:
GALVANIZED GROUP INC.

Thank you for buying our book.

Follow us on Twitter Like us on Facebook:
Galvanized Group Inc.

We'd love to hear from you: galvanizedgroupinc@gmail.com